Macmillan Paperback 48

Mavis Gallant

Overhead in a Balloon

D1431356

MACMILLAN OF CANADA

A Division of Canada Publishing Corporation
Toronto, Ontario, Canada

Copyright © 1979, 1981, 1982, 1983, 1984, 1985 by
Mavis Gallant

All rights reserved. The use of any part of this
publication, reproduced, transmitted in any form or by
any means, electronic, mechanical, photocopying,
recording, or otherwise, or stored in a retrieval system,
without the prior consent of the publisher, is an
infringement of the copyright law.

Canadian Cataloguing in Publication Data

Gallant, Mavis, date.
  Overhead in a balloon
(Macmillan paperback ; 48)
ISBN 0-7715-9961-7

I. Title.

PS8513.A593096 1990   C813'.54   C90-093053-5
PR9199.3.G35096 1990

"The Assembly" was first published in *Harper's*
magazine. All the other stories were first published in
The New Yorker.

First published in hardcover by Macmillan of Canada in
1985
First Macmillan Paperback edition 1990

Macmillan of Canada
A Division of Canada Publishing Corporation
Toronto, Ontario, Canada

Macmillan Paperbacks are distributed by
General Paperbacks, 30 Lesmill Road, Toronto, Canada M3B 2T6

Printed and bound in Canada

CONTENTS

For G. de D. M.

SPECK'S IDEA

S andor Speck's first art gallery in Paris was on the Right Bank, near the Church of St. Elisabeth, on a street too narrow for cars. When his block was wiped off the map to make way for a five-story garage, Speck crossed the Seine to the shadow of Saint-Julien-le-Pauvre, where he set up shop in a picturesque slum protected by law from demolition. When this gallery was blown up by Basque separatists, who had mistaken it for a travel agency exploiting the beauty of their coast, he collected his insurance money and moved to the Faubourg Saint-Germain.

Here, at terrifying cost, he rented four excellent rooms—two on the loggia level, and a clean dry basement for framing and storage. The entrance, particularly handsome, was on the street side of an eighteenth-century *hôtel particulier* built around an elegant court now let out as a parking concession. The building had long before been cut up into dirty, decaying apartments, whose spiteful, quarrelsome, and avaricious tenants were forgiven every failing by Speck for the sake of being the Count of this and the Prince of that. Like the flaking shutters, the rotting windowsills, the slops and oil stains in the ruined court, they bore a Proustian seal of distinction, like a warranty, making up for his insanely expensive lease. Though he appreciated style, he craved stability even more. In the Faubourg, he seemed at last likely to find it: not a stone could be removed without the approval of the toughest cultural authorities of the nation. Three Marxist embassies installed in former ducal mansions along the street required the presence of armed policemen the clock around. The only commercial establishments anywhere near Speck's—a restaurant and a bookstore—seemed unlikely targets for firebombs: the first catered to lower-echelon civil servants, the second was painted royal blue, a conservative color he found reassuring. The bookstore's name, Amandine, suggested shelves of calm regional novels and accounts of travel to Imperial Russia signed "A Diplomat." Pasted inside the window, flat on the pane, was an engraving that depicted an old man, bearded and mitred, tearing a small demon limb from limb. The old man looked self-conscious, the imp resigned. He supposed that this image concealed a deep religious meaning, which he did not intend to plumb. If it was holy, it was respectable; as the owner of the gallery across the street, he needed to know nothing more.

Speck was now in the parish of St. Clotilde, near enough to the church for its bells to give him migraine headache. Leaves from the church square blew as far as his door—melancholy reminders of autumn, a season bad for art. (Winter was bad, too, while the first chestnut leaves unfolding heralded the worst season of all. In summer the gallery closed.) In spite of his constant proximity to churches he had remained rational. Generations of highly intellectual Central European agnostics and freethinkers had left in his bones a mistrust of the bogs and quicksands that lie beyond reality perceived. Neither loss nor grief nor guilt nor fear had ever moved him to appeal to the unknown—any unknown, for there were several. Nevertheless, after signing his third lease in seven years, he decided to send Walter, his Swiss assistant, a lapsed Calvinist inching toward Rome, to light a candle at St.

Clotilde's. Walter paid for a five-franc taper and set it before St. Joseph, the most reliable intermediary he could find: a wave of post-conciliar puritanism seemed to have broken at St. Clotilde's, sweeping away most of the mute and obliging figures to whom desires and gratitude could be expressed. Walter was willing to start again in some livelier church—Notre Dame de Paris, for instance—but Speck thought enough was enough.

On a damp October evening about a year after this, there could be seen in Speck's window a drawing of a woman drying her feet (Speck permanent collection); a poster announcing the current exhibition, "Paris and Its Influence on the Tirana School, 1931-2"; five catalogues displayed attractively; and the original of the picture on the poster—a shameless copy of Foujita's "Mon Intérieur" re-entitled "Balkan Alarm Clock." In defiance of a government circular reminding Paris galleries about the energy crisis Speck had left the lights on. This was partly to give the lie to competitors who might be putting it about that he was having money troubles. He had set the burglar alarm, bolted the security door, and was now cranking down an openwork iron screen whose Art Nouveau loops and fronds allowed the works inside to be seen but nothing larger than a mouse to get in. The faint, floating sadness he always felt while locking up had to do with the time. In his experience, love affairs and marriages perished between seven and eight o'clock, the hour of rain and no taxis. All over Paris couples must be parting forever, leaving like debris along the curbs the shreds of cancelled restaurant dates, useless ballet tickets, hopeless explanations, and scraps of pride; and toward each of these disasters a taxi was pulling in, the only taxi for miles, the light on its roof already dimmed in anticipation to the twin dots that in Paris mean "occupied." But occupied by whom?

"You take it."

"No, you. You're the one in a hurry."

The lover abandoned under a dripping plane tree would feel a damp victory of a kind, awarding himself a first-class trophy for selfless behavior. It would sustain him ten seconds, until the departing one rolled down the taxi window to hurl her last flint: "You Fascist!" Why was this always the final shot, the coup de grâce delivered by women? Speck's wife, Henriette, book critic on an uncompromising political weekly, had said it three times last spring—here, in the street, where Speck stood locking the iron screen into place. He had been uneasily conscious of his wellborn neighbors, hanging out their windows, not missing a thing. Henriette had then gone away in a cab to join her lover, leaving Speck, the gallery, her job—everything that mattered.

He mourned Henriette; he missed her steadying influence. Her mind was like a one-way thoroughfare, narrow and flat, maintained in repair. As he approached the age of forty he felt that his own intellect needed not just a direction but retaining walls. Unless his thoughts were nailed down by gallery business they tended to glide away to the swamps of imagination, behind which stretched the steamier marshland of metaphysics. Confessing this to Henriette was unlikely to bring her back. There had been something brisk and joyous about her going—her hailing of a taxi as though of a friend, her surprised smile as the third "Fascist!" dissolved in the April night like a double stroke from the belfry of St. Clotilde's. He supposed he would never see her again now, except by accident. Perhaps, long after he had forgotten Henriette, he would overhear someone saying in a restaurant, "Do you see that poor mad intellectual talking to herself in the corner? That is Henriette, Sandor Speck's second wife. Of course, she was very different then; Speck kept her in shape."

While awaiting this sop, which he could hardly call consolation, he had Walter and the gallery. Walter had been with him five years—longer than either of his marriages. They had been years of spiritual second-thinking for Walter and of strain and worry for Speck. Walter in search of the Eternal was like one of those solitary skippers who set out to cross an ocean only to capsize when barely out of port. Speck had been obliged to pluck his assistant out of Unitarian waters and set him on the firm shore of the Trinity. He had towed him to Transubstantiation and back; had charted the shoals and perils of careless prayer. His own aversion to superstitious belief made Speck particularly scrupulous; he would not commit himself on Free Will, for instance, uncertain if it was supposed to be an uphill trudge wearing tight boots or a downhill slide sitting on a tea tray. He would lie awake at night planning Walter's dismissal, only to develop a traumatic chest cold if his assistant seemed restless.

"What will the gallery do without you?" he would ask on the very morning he had been meaning to say, "Walter, sit down, please. I've got something to tell you." Walter would remind him about saints and holy men who had done without everything, while Speck would envision the pure hell of having to train someone new.

On a rainy night such as this, the street resembled a set in a French film designed for export, what with the policemen's white rain capes aesthetically gleaming and the lights of the bookstore, the restaurant, and the gallery reflected, quivering, in European-looking puddles. In reality, Speck thought, there was not even hope for a subplot. Henriette had gone forever. Walter's mission could not be photographed. The owner of the restaurant was in his eighties; the waiters were poised on the brink of retirement. As for the bookseller, M. Alfred Chassepoule, he seemed to spend most of his time wiping blood off the collected speeches of Mussolini, bandaging customers, and sweeping up glass. The fact was that Amandine's had turned out to have a fixed Right Wing viewpoint, which made it subject to attack by commandos wielding iron bars. Speck, who had chosen the street for its upper-class hush, had grown used to the hoarse imprecation of the Left and shriller keening of the Right; he could tell the sob of an ambulance from the wail of a police van. The commerce of art is without bias: when insurance inspectors came round to ask what Speck might have seen, he invariably replied, "Seen where?," to which Walter, unsolicited, would add, "And I am Swiss."

Since Henriette's departure, Speck often ate his meals in the local restaurant, which catered to his frugal tastes, his vegetarian principles, and his desire to be left in peace. On the way, he would pause outside Amandine's, just enough to mark the halt as a comforting bachelor habit. He would glance over the second-hand books, the yellowing pamphlets, and the overpriced cartoons. The tone of the window display seemed old-fashioned rather than dangerous, though he knew that the slogan crowning the arrangement, "Europe for Europeans," echoed from a dark political valley. But even that valley had been full of strife and dissension and muddle, for hadn't the Ur-Fascists, the Italian ones, been in some way against an all-Europe? At least, some of their poets were. But who could take any of that seriously now? Nothing political had ever struck Speck as being above the level of a low-grade comic strip. On the cover of one volume, Uncle Sam shook hands with the Russian Bear over prostrate Europe, depicted as a maiden in a dead faint. A drawing of a spider on a field of banknotes (twelve hundred francs with frame, nine hundred without) jostled the image of a crablike hand clawing away at the map of France. Pasted against the pane, survivor of uncounted assaults, the old man continued to dismember his captive imp. Walter had told Speck he believed the old man to be St. Amand, Apostle of Flanders, Bishop in 430. "Or perhaps," said Walter, after thinking it over, "435." The imp probably stood for Flemish paganism, which the Apostle had been hard put to it to overcome.

From the rainy street Speck could see four or five of Amandine's customers—all men; he had never noticed a woman in the place—standing, reading, books held close to their noses. They had the weak eyes, long chins, and sparse, sparrow-colored hair he associated with low governmental salaries. He imagined them living with grim widowed mothers whose company they avoided after work. He had seen them, or young men like them, staggering out of the store, cut by flying glass, kicked and beaten as they lay stunned on the pavement; his anxious imagination had set them on their feet, booted and belted, the right signal given at last, swarming across to the gallery, determined to make Speck pay for injuries inflicted on them by total strangers. He saw his only early Chagall (quite likely authentic) ripped from its frame; Walter, his poor little spectacles smeared with blood, lambasted with the complete Charles Maurras, fourteen volumes, full morocco; Speck himself, his ears offended by acute Right Wing cries of "Down with foreign art!," attempting a quick counter-stroke with *Significant Minor French Realists, Twentieth Century*, which was thick enough to stun an ox. Stepping back from the window, Speck saw his own smile reflected. It was pinched and tight, and he looked a good twenty years older than thirty-nine.

His restaurant, crammed with civil servants at noon, was now nearly empty. A smell of lunchtime pot roast hung in the air. He made for his own table, from which he could see the comforting lights of the gallery. The waiter, who had finally stopped asking how Henriette was liking Africa, brought his dinner at once, setting out like little votive offerings the raw-carrot salad, the pot-roast vegetables without the meat, the quarter ounce of low-fat cheese, and a small pear. It had long been established that Speck did not wish to be disturbed by the changing of plates. He extracted a yellow pad and three pencils from his briefcase and placed them within the half circle of dishes. Speck was preparing his May-June show.

The right show at the right time: it was trickier than getting married to the right person at any time. For about a year now, Paris critics had been hinting at something missing from the world of art. These hints, poignant and patriotic on the right, neo-nationalist and pugnacious on the Left, wistful but insistent

dead Center, were all in essence saying the same thing: "The
time has come." The time had come; the hour had struck; the
moment was ripe for a revival of reason, sanity, and taste. Surely
there was more to art than this sickness, this transatlantic blight?
Fresh winds were needed to sweep the museums and galleries.
Two days ago there had been a disturbing article in *Le Monde*
(front page, lower middle, turn to page 26) by a man who never
took up his pen unless civilization was in danger. Its title,
"Redemption Through Art—Last Hope for the West?," had
been followed by other disturbing questions: When would the
merchants and dealers, compared rather unfairly to the money-
changers driven from the temple, face up to their share of
responsibility as the tattered century declined? Must the flowering gardens of Western European culture wilt and die along with
the decadent political systems, the exhausted parliaments, the
shambling elections, the tired liberal impulses? What of the man
in the street, too modest and confused to mention his cravings?
Was he not gasping for one remedy and one only—artistic
renovation? And where was this to come from? "In the words of
Shakespr," the article concluded, supposedly in English, "That is
the qustn."

As it happened, Speck had the answer: say, a French painter,
circa 1864-1949, forgotten now except by a handful of devoted
connoisseurs. Populist yet refined, local but universal, he would
send rays, beacons, into the thickening night of the West, just as
Speck's gallery shone bravely into the dark street. Speck picked
up a pencil and jotted rapidly: "Born in France, worked in Paris,
went his own way, unmindful of fashion, knowing his hour
would strike, his vision be vindicated. Catholical, as this retrospective so eloquently. . ." Just how does "catholical" come in,
Speck wondered, forking up raw carrots. Because of ubiquity, the
ubiquity of genius? No; not genius—leave that for the critics. His
sense of harmony, then—his discretion.

Easy, Speck told himself. Easy on the discretion. This isn't
interior decoration.

He could see the notices, knew which of the critics would write "At last," and "It has taken Sandor Speck to remind us." Left, Right, and Center would unite on a single theme: how the taste of two full generations had been corrupted by foreign speculation, cosmopolitan decadence, and the cultural imperialism of the Anglo-Saxon hegemony.

"The calm agnostic face," Speck wrote happily, "the quiet Cartesian voice are replaced by the snarl of a nation betrayed (1914), as startling for the viewer as a child's glimpse of a beloved adult in a temper tantrum. The snarl, the grimace vanish (1919) as the serene observer of Universal Will (1929) and of Man's responsibility to himself return. But we are left shaken. We have stopped trusting our feelings. We have been shown not only the smile but the teeth."

Here Speck drew a wavy line and turned to the biography, which was giving him trouble. On a fresh yellow page he tried again:

1938—Travels to Nice. Sees Mediterranean.
1939—Abandons pacifist principle. Lies about age. Is mobilized.
1940—Demobilized.
1941—

It was here that Speck bogged down. Should he say, "Joins Resistance"? "Resistance" today meant either a heroic moment sadly undervalued by the young or a minor movement greatly inflated in order to absolve French guilt. Whatever it is, thought Speck, it is not chic. The youngest survivor must be something like seventy-three. They know nothing about art, and never subscribe to anything except monuments. Some people read "Resistance" in a chronology and feel quite frankly exasperated. On the other hand, what about museums, state-subsidized, Resistance-minded on that account? He chewed a boiled leek and suddenly wrote, "1941—Conversations with Albert Camus." I wonder where all this comes from, Speck said to himself. Inspiration was what he meant.

These notes, typed by Walter, would be turned over to the

fashionable historian, the alarming critic, the sound political figure unlikely to be thrown out of office between now and spring, whom Speck would invite to write the catalogue introduction. "Just a few notes," Speck would say tactfully. "Knowing how busy you are." Nothing was as inspiriting to him as the thought of his own words in print on a creamy catalogue page, even over someone else's name.

Speck took out of his briefcase the Directoire snuffbox Henriette had given him about a fortnight before suddenly calling him "Fascist." (Unexpected feminine generosity—first firm sign of adulterous love affair.) It contained three after-dinner tablets—one to keep him alert until bedtime, another to counter the stimulating effect of the first, and a third to neutralize the germ known as Warsaw flu now ravaging Paris, emptying schools and factories and creating delays in the postal service. He sat quietly, digesting, giving the pills a chance to work.

He could see the structure of the show, the sketchbooks and letters in glass cases. It might be worthwhile lacquering the walls black, concentrating strong spots on the correspondence, which straddled half a century, from Degas to Cocteau. The scrawl posted by Drieu la Rochelle just before his suicide would be particularly effective on black. Céline was good; all that crowd was back in vogue now. He might use the early photo of Céline in regimental dress uniform with a splendid helmet. Of course, there would be word from the Left, too, with postcards from Jean Jaurès, Léon Blum, and Paul Éluard, and a jaunty get-well message from Louis Aragon and Elsa. In the first room Speck would hang the stiff, youthful landscapes and the portraits of the family, the artist's first models—his brother wearing a sailor suit, the awkward but touching likeness of his sister ("Germaine-Isabelle at the Window").

"Yes, yes," Speck would hear in the buzz of voices at the opening. "Even from the beginning you can tell there was *something*." The "something" became bolder, firmer in the second room. See his cities; watch how the streets turn into mazes, nets, prison corridors. Dark palette. Opaqueness, the whole canvas covered, immensities of indigo and black. "Look, 1929; he was doing it before What's-His-Name." Upstairs, form breaking out of shadow: bread, cheese, wine, wheat, ripe apples, grapes.

Hold it, Speck told himself. Hold the ripeness. This isn't social realism.

He gathered up the pencils, the snuffbox, and the pad, and put them back in the briefcase. He placed seventy francs, tip included, in a saucer. Still he sat, his mind moving along to the second loggia room, the end room, the important one. Here on the neutral walls would be the final assurance, the serenity, the satire, the power, and the vision for which, at last, the time had come. For that was the one thing Speck was sure of: the bell had rung, the hour had struck, the moment was at hand.

Whose time? Which hour? Yes—whose, which, what? That was where he was stuck.

The street was now empty except for the policemen in their streaming capes. The bookstore had put up its shutter. Speck observed the walls of the three Marxist embassies. Shutters and curtains that once had shielded the particular privacy of the aristocracy—privacy open to servants but not to the street—now concealed the receptions and merry dinner parties of people's democracies. Sometimes at this hour gleaming motorcars rolled past the mysterious gates, delivering passengers Speck's fancy continued to see as the Duchesse de Guermantes and anyone she did not happen to despise. He knew that the chauffeurs were armed and that half the guests were spies; still, there was nothing to stop a foreign agent from having patrician tastes, or from admiring Speck's window as he drove by.

"This gallery will be an oasis of peace and culture," Walter had predicted as they were hanging the first show, "Little-Known Aspects of Post-Decorator Style." "An oasis of peace and culture in the international desert."

Speck breathed germ-laden night air. Boulevard theatres and music halls were deserted, their managers at home writing letters to the mayor of Paris deploring the decline of popular entertainment and suggesting remedies in the form of large cash subsidies. The sluggish river of autumn life congealed and stagnated around millions of television sets as Parisians swallowed aspirin and drank the boiling-hot Scotch believed to be a sovereign defense against Warsaw flu.

A few determined intellectuals slunk, wet, into the Métro on their way to cultural centers where, in vivid translations from the German, actors would address the occasional surly remark to the audience—that loyal, anxious, humorless audience in its costly fake working-class clothes. Another contingent, dressed in Burberry trench-coats, had already fought its way into the Geographical Institute, where a lecture with colored slides, "Ramblings in Secret Greenland," would begin, after a delay owing to trouble with the projection machine, at about nine-twenty. The advantage of slides over films was that they were not forever jumping about and confusing one, and the voice describing them belonged to a real speaker. When the lights went up, one could see him, talk to him, challenge him over the thing he had said about shamanism on Disko Island. What had drawn the crowd was not Greenland but the word "secret." In no other capital city does the population wait more trustfully for the mystery to be solved, the conspiracy laid bare, the explanation of every sort of vexation to be supplied: why money slumps, why prices climb, why it rains in August, why children are ungrateful. The answers might easily come from a man with a box of slides.

In each of the city's twenty administrative districts, Communists, distinguished by the cleanliness of their no-iron shirts, the sobriety of their washable neckties, and the modesty of their bearing, moved serenely toward their local cell meetings. I must persuade Walter to take out membership sometime, Speck thought. It might be useful and interesting for the gallery and it would take his mind off salvation.

Walter was at this moment in the Church of St. Gervais, across the Seine, where an ecumenical gathering of prayer, music, and debate on Unity of Faith had been marred the week before by ugly scuffling between middle-aged latecomers and young persons in the lotus position, taking up too much room. Walter had turned to his neighbor, a stranger to him, and asked courteously, "Is it a string ensemble tonight, or just the organ?" Mistaken for a traditionalist demanding the Latin Mass, he had been punched in the face and had to be led to a side chapel to mop up his nosebleed. God knows what they might do to him tonight, Speck thought.

As for Speck himself, nine-thirty found him in good company, briskly tying the strings of his Masonic apron. No commitment stronger than prudence kept him from being at St. Gervais, listening for a voice in the night of the soul, or at a Communist Party cell meeting, hoping to acquire a more wholesome slant on art in a doomed society, but he had already decided that only the Infinite could be everywhere at once. The Masonic Grand Architect of the Universe laid down no rules, appointed no prophets, required neither victims nor devotion, and seemed content to exist as a mere possibility. At the lodge Speck rubbed shoulders with men others had to be content to glimpse on television. He stood now no more than three feet away from Kléber Schaumberger, of the Alsatian Protestant banking Schaumbergers; had been greeted by Olivier Ombrine, who designed all the Arabian princesses' wedding gowns; could see, without craning, the plume of white hair belonging to François-Xavier Blum-Bloch-Weiler—former ambassador, historian, member of the French Academy, author of a perennially best-selling book about Vietnam called *When France Was at the Helm*. Speck kept the ambassador's family tree filed in his head. The Blum-Bloch-Weilers, heavy art collectors, produced states-

men, magistrates, anthropologists, and generals, and were on no
account to be confused with the Blum-Weiler-Blochs, their
penniless and mystical cousins, who produced poets, librarians,
and Benedictine monks.

Tonight Speck followed the proceedings mechanically; his
mind was set on the yellow pad in his briefcase, now lying on the
back seat of his car. Direct address and supplication to the
unknown were frowned on here. Order reigned in a complex
universe where the Grand Architect, insofar as he existed, was
supposed to know what he was doing. However, having nowhere
to turn, Speck decided for the first time in his life to brave
whatever cosmic derangement might ensue and to unburden
himself.

Whoever and whatever you are, said Speck silently, as many
had said before him, remember in my favor that I have never
bothered you. I never called your attention to the fake Lauren-
cin, the stolen Magritte, the Bonnard the other gallery was
supposed to have insured, the Maurice Denis notebook that
slipped through my fingers, the Vallotton woodcut that got lost
between Paris and Lausanne. All I want...But there was no
point in his insisting. The Grand Architect, if he was any sort of
omnipresence worth considering, knew exactly what Speck
needed now: he needed the tiny, enduring wheel set deep in the
clanking, churning machinery of the art trade—the artist himself.

Speck came out to the street refreshed and soothed, feeling
that he had shed some of his troubles. The rain had stopped. A
bright moon hung low. He heard someone saying, "...hats." On
the glistening pavement a group of men stood listening while
Senator Antoine Bellefeuille told a funny story. Facts from the
Bellefeuille biography tumbled through Speck's mind: twenty
years a deputy from a rich farming district, twice a Cabinet
minister, now senator; had married a sugar-beet fortune, which
he inherited when his wife died; no children; his mother had left
him majority shares in milk chocolate, which he had sold to invest
in the first postwar plastics; owned a racing stable in Normandy, a

château in Provence, one of the last fine houses of Paris; had taken first-class degrees in law and philosophy; had gone into politics almost as an afterthought.

What had kept the old man from becoming Prime Minister, even President of the Republic? He had the bearing, the brains, the fortune, and the connections. Too contented, Speck decided, observing his lodge brother by moonlight. But clever, too; he was supposed to have kept copies of files from the time he had been at Justice. He splashed around in the arts, knew the third-generation dealers, the elegant bachelor curators. He went to openings, was not afraid of new movements, but he never bought anything. Speck tried to remember why the wealthy Senator who liked art never bought pictures.

"She was stunning," the Senator said. "Any man of my generation will tell you that. She came down Boulevard Saint-Michel on her husband's arm. He barely reached her shoulder. She had a smile like a fox's. Straight little animal teeth. Thick red-gold hair. A black hat tilted over one eye. And what a throat. And what hands and arms. A waist no larger than this," said the Senator, making a circle with his hands. "As I said, in those days men wore hats. You tipped a bowler by the brim, the other sort you picked up by the crown. I was so dazzled by being near her, by having the famous Lydia Cruche smile at me, I forgot I was wearing a bowler and tried to pick it up by the crown. You can imagine what a fool I looked, and how she laughed."

And of course they laughed, and Speck laughed, too.

"Her husband," said the Senator. "Hubert Cruche. A face like a gargoyle. Premature senile dementia. He'd been kicked by Venus at some time or other"—the euphemism for syphilis. "In those days the cure was based on mercury—worse than the disease. He seemed to know me. There was light in his eyes. Oh, not the light of intelligence. It was too late for that, and he'd not had much to begin with. He recognized me for a simple reason. I had already begun to assemble my Cruche collection. I bought everything Hubert Cruche produced for sixteen years—the oils, the gouaches, the pastels, the watercolors, the etchings, the drawings, the woodcuts, the posters, the cartoons, the book illustrations. Everything."

That was it, Speck remembered. That was why the Senator who liked art never bought so much as a wash drawing. The house was full of Cruches; there wasn't an inch to spare on the walls.

With a monarch's gesture, the Senator dismissed his audience and stepped firmly toward the chauffeur, who stood holding the door of his Citroën. He said, perhaps to himself, perhaps to Speck, thin and attentive in the moonlight, "I suppose I ought to get rid of my Cruches. Who ever thinks about Cruche now?"

"No," said Speck, whom the Grand Architect of the Universe had just rapped over the head. The Senator paused—benevolent, stout. "Don't get rid of the Cruches," said Speck. He felt as if he were on a distant shore, calling across deep cultural waters. "Don't sell! Hang on! Cruche is coming back!"

Cruche, Cruche, Hubert Cruche, sang Speck's heart as he drove homeward. Cruche's hour had just struck, along with Sandor Speck's. At the core of the May-June retrospective would be his lodge brother's key collection: "Our thanks, in particular...who not only has loaned his unique and invaluable...but who also...and who...." Recalling the little he knew of Cruche's obscure career, Speck made a few changes in the imaginary catalogue, substituting with some disappointment "The Power Station at Gagny-sur-Orme" for "Misia Sert on Her Houseboat," and "Peasant Woman Sorting Turnips" for "Serge Lifar as Petrouchka." He wondered if he could call Cruche heaven-sent. No; he would not put a foot beyond coincidence, just as he had not let Walter dash from saint to saint once he had settled for St. Joseph. And yet a small flickering marsh light danced upon the low-lying metaphysical ground he had done so much to avoid. Not only did Cruche overlap to an astonishing degree the painter in the yellow notebook but he was exactly the sort of painter that made the Speck gallery chug along. If Speck's personal collection consisted of minor works by celebrated artists, he considered them his collateral for a rainy, bank-loan day. Too canny to try to compete with international heavyweights, unwilling to burden himself with insurance, he had developed as his specialty the flattest, palest, farthest ripples of the late-middle-traditional Paris school. This sensible decision had earned him the admiration given the devoted miniaturist who is no threat to anyone. "Go and see Sandor Speck," the great lions and tigers of the trade would tell clients they had no use for. "Speck's the expert."

Speck was expert on barges, bridges, cafés at twilight, nudes on striped counterpanes, the artist's mantelpiece with mirror, the artist's street, his staircase, his bed made and rumpled, his still-life with half-peeled apple, his summer in Mexico, his wife reading a book, his girlfriend naked and dejected on a kitchen chair. He knew that the attraction of customer to picture was always accidental, like love; it was his business to make it overwhelming. Visitors came to the gallery looking for decoration and investment, left it believing Speck had put them on the road to a supreme event. But there was even more to Speck than this, and if he was respected for anything in the trade it was for his knack with artists' widows. Most dealers hated them. They were considered vain, greedy, unrealistic, and tougher than bulldogs. The worst were those whose husbands had somehow managed the rough crossing to recognition only to become washed up at the wrong end of the beach. There the widow waited, guarding the wreckage. Speck's skill in dealing with them came out of a certain sympathy. An artist's widow was bound to be suspicious and adamant. She had survived the discomfort and confusion of her marriage; had lived through the artist's drinking, his avarice, his affairs, his obsession with constipation, his feuds and quarrels, his cowardice with dealers, his hypocrisy with critics, his depressions (which always fell at the most joyous seasons, blighting Christmas and spring); and then—oh, justice!—she had outlasted him.

Transfiguration arrived rapidly. Resurrected for Speck's approval was an ardent lover, a devoted husband who could not work unless his wife was around, preferably in the same room. If she had doubts about a painting, he at once scraped it down. Hers was the only opinion he had ever trusted. His last coherent words before dying had been of praise for his wife's autumnal beauty.

Like a swan in muddy waters, Speck's ancient Bentley cruised the suburbs where his painters had lived their last resentful seasons. He knew by heart the damp villa, the gravel path, the dangling bellpull, the shrubbery containing dead cats and plastic bottles. Indoors the widow sat, her walls plastered with portraits of herself when young. Here she continued the struggle begun in the Master's lifetime—the evicting of the upstairs tenant—her day made lively by the arrival of mail (dusty beige of anonymous threats, grim blue of legal documents), the coming and going of process servers, the outings to lawyers. Into this spongy territory Speck advanced, bringing his tactful presence, his subtle approximation of courtship, his gift for listening. Thin by choice, pale by nature, he suggested maternal need. Socks and cufflinks suggested breeding. The drift of his talk suggested prosperity. He sent his widows flowers, wooed them with food. Although their taste in checks and banknotes ran to the dry and crisp, when it came to eating they craved the sweet, the sticky, the moist. From the finest pastry shops in Paris Speck brought soft macaroons, savarins soaked in rum, brioches stuffed with almond cream, mocha cake so tender it had to be eaten with a spoon. Sugar was poison to Speck. Henriette had once reviewed a book that described how refined sugar taken into one's system turned into a fog of hideous green. Her brief, cool warning, "A Marxist Considers Sweets," unreeled in Speck's mind if he was confronted with a cookie. He usually pretended to eat, reducing a *mille-feuille* to paste, concealing the wreck of an éclair under napkin and fork. He never lost track of his purpose—the prying of paintings out of a dusty studio on terms anesthetizing to the artist's widow and satisfactory to himself.

The Senator had mentioned a wife; where there had been wife there was relict. Speck obtained her telephone number by calling a rival gallery and pretending to be looking for someone else. "Cruche's widow can probably tell you," he finally heard. She lived in one of the gritty suburbs east of Paris, on the far side of the Bois de Vincennes—in Speck's view, the wrong direction. The pattern of his life seemed to come unfolded as he dialled. He saw himself stalled in industrial traffic, inhaling pollution, his Bentley pointed toward the seediest mark on the urban compass, with a vanilla cream cake melting beside him on the front seat.

She answered his first ring; his widows never strayed far from the telephone. He introduced himself. Silence. He gave the name of the gallery, mentioned his street, recited the names of painters he showed.

Presently he heard "D'you know any English?"

"Some," said Speck, who was fluent.

"Well, what do you want?"

"First of all," he said, "to meet you."

"What for?"

He cupped his hand round the telephone, as if spies from the embassies down the street were trying to overhear. "I am planning a major Cruche show. A retrospective. That's what I want to talk to you about."

"Not unless I know what you want."

It seemed to Speck that he had already told her. Her voice was languid and nasal and perfectly flat. An index to English dialects surfaced in his mind, yielding nothing useful.

"It will be a strong show," he went on. "The first big Cruche since the nineteen-thirties, I believe."

"What's that got to do with me?"

He wondered if the Senator had forgotten something essential—that Lydia Cruche had poisoned her husband, for instance.

He said, "You probably own quite a lot of his work."

"None of it's for sale."

This, at last, was familiar; widows' negotiations always began with "No." "Actually, I am not proposing to buy anything," he said, wanting this to be clear at the start. "I am offering the hospitality of my gallery. It's a gamble I am willing to take because of my firm belief that the time—"

"What's the point of this show?"

"The point?" said Speck, his voice tightening as it did when Walter was being obtuse. "The point is getting Cruche back on the market. The time has come—the time to...to attack. To attack the museums with Hubert Cruche."

As he said this, Speck saw the great armor-plated walls of the Pompidou Art Center and the chink in the armor through which an 80 x 95 Cruche 1919 abstract might slip. He saw the provincial museums, cheeseparing, saving on light bulbs, but, like the French bourgeoisie they stood for, so much richer than they seemed. At the name "Cruche" their curators would wake up from neurotic dreams of forced auction sales, remembering they had millions to get rid of before the end of the fiscal year. And France was the least of it; London, Zurich, Stockholm, and Amsterdam materialized as frescoes representing the neoclassical façades of four handsome banks. Overhead, on a Baroque ceiling, nymphs pointed their rosy feet to gods whose chariots were called "Tokyo" and "New York." Speck lowered his voice as if he had portentous news. Museums all over the world, although they did not yet know this, were starving for Cruche. In the pause that followed he seemed to feel Henriette's hand on his shoulder, warning him to brake before enthusiasm took him over the cliff.

"Although for the moment Cruche is just an idea of mine," he said, stopping cold at the edge. "Just an idea. We can develop the idea when we meet."

A week later, Speck parked his car between a ramshackle shopping center—survivor of the building boom of the sixties—and a municipal low-cost housing project that resembled a jail. In the space bounded by these structures crouched the late artist's villa, abiding proof in stucco that the taste of earlier generations had been as disastrous as today's. He recognized the shards of legal battle: center and block had left the drawing board of some state-employed hack as a unit, only to be wedged apart by a widow's refusal to sell. Speck wondered how she had escaped expropriation. Either she knows someone powerful, he thought, or she can make such a pest of herself that they were thankful to give up.

A minute after having pushed the gate and tugged the rusted wire bellpull, he found himself alone in a bleak sitting room, from which his hostess had been called by a whistling kettle. He sat down on a faded sofa. The furniture was of popular local design, garnished with marble and ormolu. A television set encrusted with gilt acanthus leaves sat on a sideboard, like an objet d'art. A few rectangular shadings on the wallpaper showed where pictures had hung.

The melancholy tinged with foreboding Speck felt between seven and eight overtook him at this much earlier hour. The room was no more hideous than others he had visited in his professional quest for a bargain, but this time it seemed to daunt him, recalling sieges and pseudo courtships and expenditures of time, charm, and money that had come to nothing. He got up and examined a glass-fronted bookcase with nothing inside. His features, afloat on a dusty pane, were not quite as pinched as they had been the other night, but the image was still below par for a man considered handsome. The approach of a squeaking tea cart sent him scurrying back to the sofa, like a docile child invited somewhere for the first time.

"I was just admiring..." he began.

"I've run out of milk," she said. "I'm sure you won't mind your tea plain." With this governessy statement she handed him a cup of black Ceylon, a large slice of poisonous raisin cake, and a Mickey Mouse paper napkin.

Nothing about Cruche's widow tallied with the Senator's

description. She was short and quite round, and reminded Speck of the fat little dogs one saw being reluctantly exercised in Paris streets. The abundant red-gold hair of the Senator's memory, or imagination, had gone ash-gray and was, in any case, pinned up. The striking fact of her person was simply the utter blankness of her expression. Usually widows' faces spoke to him. They said, "I am lonely," or "Can I trust you?" Lydia Cruche's did not suggest that she had so much as taken Speck in. She chose a chair at some distance from Speck, and proceeded to eat her cake without speaking. He thought of things to say, but none of them seemed appealing.

At last, she said, "Did you notice the supermarket next door?"

"I saw a shopping center."

"The market is part of it. You can get anything there now— bran, frozen pizzas, maple syrup. That's where I got the cake mix. I haven't been to Paris for three years."

Speck had been born in France. French education had left him the certainty that he was a logical, fair-minded person imbued with a culture from which every other Western nation was obliged to take its bearings. French was his first language; he did not really approve of any other. He said, rather coldly, "Have you been in this country long?"

"Around fifty years."

"Then you should know some French."

"I don't speak it if I don't have to. I never liked it."

He put down his cup, engulfed by a wave of second-generation distress. She was his first foreign widow. Most painters, whatever their origins, had sense enough to marry French- women—unrivalled with creditors, thrifty hoarders of bits of real estate, endowed with relations in country places where one could decamp in times of need and war.

"Perhaps, where you come from—" he began.

"Saskatchewan."

His tea had gone cold. Tannic scum had collected on its surface. She said, "This idea of yours, this show—what was it you called it? The hospitality of your gallery? I just want to say don't count on me. Don't count on me for anything. I don't mind showing you what I've got. But not today. The studio hasn't been dusted or heated for years, and even the light isn't working."

In Speck's experience, this was about average for a first attempt. Before making for civilization he stopped at a florist's in the shopping center and ordered two dozen roses to be delivered to Mme. Cruche. While these were lifted, dripping, from a plastic pail, he jotted down a warm message on his card, crossing out the engraved "Dr. Sandor Speck." His title, earned by a thesis on French neo-Humanism and its ups and downs, created some confusion in Paris, where it was taken to mean that Speck could cure slipped discs and gastric ulcers. Still, he felt that it gave a grip to his name, and it was his only link with all the freethinking, agnostic Specks, who, though they had not been able to claim affinity by right of birth with Voltaire and Descartes, had probably been wise and intelligent and quite often known as "Dr."

As soon as he got back to the gallery, he had Walter look up Saskatchewan in an atlas. Its austere oblong shape turned his heart to ice. Walter said that it was one of the right-angled territories that so frequently contain oil. Oil seemed to Speck to improve the oblong. He saw a Chirico chessboard sliding off toward a horizon where the lights of derricks twinkled and blinked.

H e let a week go by before calling Lydia Cruche.

"I won't be able to show you those roses of yours," she said. "They died right off."

He took the hint and arrived with a spray of pale-green orchids imported from Brazil. Settled upon the faded sofa, which was apparently destined to be his place, he congratulated his hostess on the discovery of oil in her native plain.

"I haven't seen or heard of the place since Trotsky left the

Soviet Union," she said. "If there is oil, I'd sooner not know about it. Oil is God's curse." The iron silence that followed this seemed to press on Speck's lungs. "That's a bad cough you've got there, Doctor," she said. "Men never look after those things. Who looks after you?"

"I look after myself," said Speck.

"Where's your wife? Where'd she run off to?"

Not even "Are you married?" He saw his hostess as a tough little pagan figure, with a goddess's gift for reading men's lives. He had a quick vision of himself clasping her knees and sobbing out the betrayal of his marriage, though he continued to sit upright, crumbling walnut cake so that he would not have to eat it.

"My wife," he said, "insofar as I can still be said to have one, has gone to live in a warm climate."

"She run off alone? Women don't often do that. They haven't got that kind of nerve."

Stepping carefully, for he did not wish to sound like a stage cuckold or a male fool, Speck described in the lightest possible manner how Henriette had followed her lover, a teacher of literature, to a depressed part of French-speaking Africa where the inhabitants were suffering from a shortage of Racine. Unable to halt once he had started, he tore on toward the edge: Henriette was a hopeless nymphomaniac (she had fallen in love) who lacked any sense of values (the man was broke); she was at the same time a grasping neurotic (having sunk her savings in the gallery, she wanted a return with fourteen per cent interest).

"You must be thankful you finally got rid of her," said Lydia Cruche. "You must be wondering why you married her in the first place."

"I felt sorry for Henriette," he said, momentarily forgetting any other reason. "She seemed so helpless." He told about Henriette living in her sixth-floor walkup, working as slave labor on a shoddy magazine. A peasant from Alsace, she had never eaten anything but pickled cabbage until Speck drove his Bentley

into her life. Under his tactful guidance she had tasted her first
fresh truffle salad at Le Récamier; had worn her first mink-lined
Dior raincoat; had published her first book-length critical essay,
"A Woman Looks at Edgar Allan Poe." And then she had left
him—just like that.

"You trained her," said Lydia Cruche. "Brought her up to
your level. And now she's considered good enough to marry a
teacher. You should feel proud. You shouldn't mind what
happened. You should feel satisfied."

"I'm not satisfied," said Speck. "I do mind." He realized that
something had been left out of his account. "I loved her." Lydia
Cruche looked straight at him, for once, as though puzzled. "As
you loved Hubert Cruche," he said.

There was no response except for the removal of crumbs from
her lap. The goddess, displeased by his mortal impertinence,
symbolically knocked his head off her knee.

"Hube liked my company," she finally said. "That's true
enough. After he died I saw him sitting next to the television, by
the radiator, where his mother usually crouched all winter
looking like a sheep with an earache. I was just resting here,
thinking of nothing in particular, when I looked up and noticed
him. He said, 'You carry the seed of your death.' I said, 'If that's
the case, I might as well put my head in the oven and be done
with it.' 'Non,' he said, 'ce n'est pas la peine.' Now, his mother
was up in her room, making lists of all the things she had to feel
sorry about. I went up and said, 'Madame,' because you can bet
your boots she never got a 'Maman' out of me, 'Hube was in the
parlor just now.' She answered, 'It was his mother he wanted.
Any message was for me.' I said that if that was so, then all he
needed to do was to materialize upstairs and save me the bother
of climbing. She gave me some half-baked reason why he
preferred not to, and then she *did* die. Aged a hundred and three.
It was in *France-Soir*."

The French she had spoken rang to Speck like silver bells.
Everything about her had changed—voice, posture, expression.

If he still could not see the Lydia Cruche of the Senator's vision, at least he could believe in her.

"Do you talk to your husband often?" he said, trying to make it sound like a usual experience.

"How could I talk to Hube? He's dead and buried. I hope you don't go in for ghosts, Dr. Speck. I would find that very silly. That was just some kind of accident—a visitation. I never saw him again or ever expect to. As for his mother, there wasn't a peep out of her after she died. And here I am, alone in the Cruche house." It was hard to say if she sounded glad or sorry. "I gather you're on your own, too. God never meant men and women to live by themselves, convenient though it may seem to some of us. That's why he throws men and women together. Coincidence is God's plan."

So soon, thought Speck. It was only their second meeting. It seemed discourteous to draw attention to the full generation that lay between them; experience had taught him that acknowledging any fragment of this dangerous subject did more harm than good. When widows showed their cards, he tried to look like a man with no time for games. He thought of the young André Malraux, dark and tormented, the windblown lock on the worried brow, the stub of a Gauloise sending up a vagabond spiral of smoke. Unfortunately, Speck had been born forty years too late for the model; he belonged to a much reedier generation of European manhood. He thought of the Pope. White-clad, serene, he gazed out on St. Peter's Square, over the subdued heads of one hundred thousand artists' widows, not one of whom would dare.

"So this was the Cruche family home," he said, striking out, he hoped, in a safe direction.

"The furniture was his mother's," said Lydia Cruche. "I got rid of most of it, but there was stuff you couldn't pay them to cart away. *Sa petite Maman adorable*," she said softly. Again Speck heard the string of silver bells. "I thought she was going to hang around forever. They were a tough family—peasants from the west of France. She took good care of him. Cooked him sheep's

heart, tripe and onions, big beefsteaks they used to eat half raw.
He was good-looking, a big fellow, big for a Frenchman. At
seventy you'd have taken him for forty. Never had a cold. Never
had a headache. Never said he was tired. Drank a litre of
Calvados every other day. One morning he just keeled over, and
that was that. I'll show you a picture of him sometime."

"I'd also like to see *his* pictures," said Speck, thankful for the
chance. "The pictures you said you had upstairs."

"You know how I met Hube? People often ask me that. I'm
surprised you haven't. I came to him for lessons."

"I didn't know he taught," said Speck. His most reliable
professional trait was his patience.

"He didn't. I admired him so much that I thought I'd try
anyway. I was eighteen. I rang the bell. His mother let me in. I
never left—he wouldn't let me go. His mother often said if she'd
known the future she'd never have answered the door. I must
have walked about four miles from a tram stop, carrying a big
portfolio of my work to show him. There wasn't even a paved
street then—just a patch of nettles out front and some vacant
lots."

Her work. He knew he had to get it over with: "Would you
like to show me some of your things, too?"

"I burned it all a long time ago."

Speck's heart lurched. "But not his work?"

"It wasn't mine to burn. I'm not a criminal." Mutely, he
looked at the bare walls. "None of Hube's stuff ever hung in
here," she said. "His mother couldn't stand it. We had everything *she* liked—Napoleon at Waterloo, lighthouses, corona-
tions. I couldn't touch it when she was alive, but once she'd gone
I didn't wait two minutes."

Speck's eighteenth-century premises were centrally heated.
The system, which dated from the early nineteen-sixties,
had been put in by Americans who had once owned most of the

second floor. With the first dollar slide of the Nixon era they had wisely sold their holdings and gone home, without waiting for the calamity still to come. Their memorial was an expensive, casual gift nobody knew what to do with; it had raised everyone's property taxes, and it cost a fortune to run. Tenants, such as Speck, who paid a fat share of the operation, had no say as to when heat was turned on, or to what degree of temperature. Only owners and landlords had a vote. They voted overwhelmingly for the lowest possible fuel bills. By November there was scarcely a trace of warmth in Speck's elegant gallery, his cold was entrenched for the winter, and Walter was threatening to quit. Speck was showing a painter from Bruges, sponsored by a Belgian cultural-affairs committee. Cost-sharing was not a habit of his—it lowered the prestige of the gallery—but in a tight financial season he sometimes allowed himself a breather. The painter, who clearly expected Speck to put him under contract, talked of moving to Paris.

"You'd hate it here," said Speck.

Belgian television filmed the opening. The Belgian royal family, bidden by Walter, on his own initiative, sent regrets signed by aides-de-camp on paper so thick it would scarcely fold. These were pinned to the wall, and drew more attention than the show itself. Only one serious critic turned up. The rooms were so cold that guests could not write their names in the visitors' book— their hands were too numb. Walter, perhaps by mistake, had invited Blum-Weiler-Blochs instead of Blum-Bloch-Weilers. They came in a horde, leading an Afghan hound they tried to raffle off for charity.

The painter now sat in the gallery, day after day, smoking black cigarettes that smelled of mutton stew. He gave off a deep professional gloom, which affected Walter. Walter began to speak of the futility of genius—a sure sign of melancholia. Speck gave the painter money so that he could smoke in cafés. The bells of St. Clotilde's clanged and echoed, saying to Speck's memory, "Fascist, Fascist, Fascist." Walter reminded Speck that November was bad for art. The painter returned from a café looking cheerful. Speck wondered if he was enjoying Paris and if he would decide to stay; he stopped giving him money and the gallery became once more infested with mutton stew and despair. Speck began a letter to Henriette imploring her to come back. Walter interrupted it with the remark that Rembrandt, Mozart, and Dante had lived in vain. Speck tore the letter up and started another one saying that a Guillaumin pastel was missing and suggesting that Henriette had taken it to Africa. Just as he was tearing this up, too, the telephone rang.

"I finally got Hube's stuff all straightened out," said Lydia Cruche. "You might as well come round and look at it this afternoon. By the way, you may call me 'Lydia,' if you want to."

"Thank you," said Speck. "And you, of course, must call me—"

"I wouldn't dream of it. Once a doctor always a doctor. Come early. The light goes at four."

Speck took a pill to quiet the pounding of his heart.

In her summing-up of his moral nature, a compendium that had preceded her ringing "Fascist"'s, Henriette had declared that Speck appraising an artist's work made her think of a real-estate loan officer examining Chartres Cathedral for leaks. It was true that his feeling for art stopped short of love; it had to. The great cocottes of history had shown similar prudence. Madame de Pompadour had eaten vanilla, believed to arouse the senses, but such recklessness was rare. Cool but efficient—that was the professional ticket. No vanilla for Speck; he knew better. For what if he were to allow passion for painting to set alight his common sense? How would he be able to live then, knowing that the ultimate fate of art was to die of anemia in safe-deposit vaults? Ablaze with love, he might try to organize raids and rescue parties, dragging pictures out of the dark, leaving sacks of onions instead. He might drop the art trade altogether, as Walter kept intending to do, and turn his talents to cornering the onion market. The same customers would ring at election time, saying, "Dr. Speck, what happens to my onion collection if the Left gets in? Shouldn't we try to unload part of it in New York now, just to be on the safe side?" And Speck, unloading onions of his own in Tokyo, would answer, "Don't worry. They can't possibly nationalize all the onions. Besides, they aren't going to win."

Lydia seemed uninterested in Speck's reaction to Cruche. He had expected her to hang about, watching his face, measuring his interest, the better to nail her prices; but she simply showed him a large, dim, dusty, north-facing room in which canvases were thickly stacked against the walls and said, "I wasn't able to get the light fixed. I've left a lamp. Don't knock it over. Tea will be ready when you are." Presently he heard American country music rising from the kitchen (Lydia must have been tuned to the BBC) and he smelled a baking cake. Then, immersed in his ice-cold Cruche encounter, he noticed nothing more.

About three hours later he came downstairs, slowly, wiping dust from his hands with a handkerchief. His conception of the show had been slightly altered, and for the better, by the total Cruche. He began to rewrite the catalogue notes: "The time has come for birth ..." No—"for rebirth. In a world sated by overstatement the moment is ripe for a calm ..." How to avoid "statement" and still say "statement"? The Grand Architect was keeping Speck in mind. "For avouchment," said Speck, alone on the stairs. It was for avouchment that the time had come. It was also here for hard business. His face became set and distant, as if a large desk were about to be shoved between Lydia Cruche and himself.

He sat down and said, "This is going to be a strong show, a powerful show, even stronger than I'd hoped. Does everything I've looked at upstairs belong to you outright? Is there anything which for any reason you are not allowed to lend, show, or sell?"

"Neither a borrower nor a lender be," said Lydia, cutting caramel cake.

"No. Well, I am talking about the show, of course."

"No show," she said. "I already told you that."

"What do you mean, no show?" said Speck.

"What I told you at the beginning. I told you not to count on me. Don't drop boiled frosting on your trousers. I couldn't get it to set."

"But you changed your mind," said Speck. "After saying 'Don't count on me,' you changed your mind."

"Not for a second."

"Why?" said Speck, as he had said to the departing Henriette. "Why?"

"God doesn't want it."

He waited for more. She folded her arms and stared at the blank television set. "How do you know that God doesn't want Hubert Cruche to have a retrospective?"

"Because He said so."

His first thought was that the Grand Architect had granted Lydia Cruche something so far withheld from Sandor Speck: a plain statement of intention. "Don't you know your Commandments?" she asked. "You've never heard of the graven image?"

He searched her face for the fun, the teasing, even the malice that might give shape to this conversation, allow him to take hold of it. He said, "I can't believe you mean this."

"You don't have to. I'm sure you have your own spiritual pathway. Whatever it is, I respect it. God reveals himself according to each person's mental capacity."

One of Speck's widows could prove she descended from Joan of Arc. Another had spent a summer measuring the walls of Toledo in support of a theory that Jericho had been in Spain. It was Speck's policy never to fight the current of eccentricity but to float with it. He said cautiously, "We are all held in a mysterious hand." Generations of Speck freethinkers howled from their graves; he affected not to hear them.

"I am a Japhethite, Dr. Speck. You remember who Noah was? And his sons, Ham, Shem, and Japheth? What does that mean to you?" Speck looked as if he possessed Old Testament lore too fragile to stand exposure. "Three," said Lydia. "The sacred number. The first, the true, the only source of Israel. That crowd Moses led into the desert were just Egyptian malcontents. The true Israelites were scattered all over the earth by then. The Bible hints at this for its whole length. Japheth's people settled in Scotland. Present-day Jews are impostors."

"Are you connected to this Japheth?"

"I do not make that claim. My Scottish ancestors came from the border country. The Japhethites had been driven north long before by the Roman invasion. The British Israelite movement, which preceded ours, proved that the name 'Hebrides' was primitive Gaelic for 'Hebrew.' The British Israelites were distinguished pathfinders. It was good of you to have come all the way out here, Dr. Speck. I imagine you'll want to be getting back."

After backing twice into Lydia's fence, Speck drove straight to Galignani's bookshop, on Rue de Rivoli, where he purchased an English Bible. He intended to have Walter ransack it for contra-Japhethite pronouncements. The orange dust jacket surprised him; it seemed to Speck that Bibles were usually black. On the back flap the churches and organizations that had sponsored this English translation were listed, among them the National Bible Society of Scotland. He wondered if this had anything to do with Japheth.

As far as Speck could gather from passages Walter marked during the next few days, art had never really flourished, even before Moses decided to put a stop to it. Apart from a bronze snake cast at God's suggestion (Speck underscored this for Lydia in red), there was nothing specifically cultural, though Ezekiel's visions had a certain surrealistic splendor. As Speck read the words "the terrible crystal," its light flooded his mind, illuminating a simple question: Why not forget Hubert Cruche and find an easier solution for the cultural penury of the West? The crystal dimmed. Speck's impulsive words that October night,

"Cruche is coming back," could not be reeled in. Senator Bellefeuille was entangled in a promise that had Speck at one end and Lydia at the other. Speck had asked if he might examine his lodge brother's collection and had been invited to lunch. Cruche *had* to come back.

Believing Speck's deliverance at hand, Walter assailed him with texts and encouragement. He left Biblical messages on Speck's desk so that he had to see them first thing after lunch. Apparently the British Israelite movement had truly existed, enjoying a large and respectable following. Its premise that it was the British who were really God's elect had never been challenged, though membership had dwindled at mid-century; Walter could find no trace of Lydia's group, however. He urged Speck to drive to the north of Scotland, but Speck had already decided to abandon the religious approach to Cruche.

"No modern translation conveys the word of Japheth or of God," Lydia had said when Speck showed her Walter's finds. There had been something unusual about the orange dust jacket, after all. He did not consider this a defeat. Bible reading had raised his spirits. He understood now why Walter found it consoling, for much in it consisted of the assurance of downing one's enemies, dashing them against stones, seeing their children reduced to beggary and their wives to despair. Still, he was not drawn to deep belief: he remained rational, skeptical, anxious, and subject to colds, and he had not succeeded in moving Lydia Cruche an inch.

Lunch at Senator Bellefeuille's was balm. Nothing was served that Speck could not swallow. From the dining room he looked across at the dark November trees of the Bois de Boulogne. The Senator lived on the west side of Paris—the clients' side. A social allegory in the shape of a city separated Speck from Lydia Cruche. The Senator's collection was fully insured, free from dust, attractively framed or stored in racks built to order.

Speck began a new catalogue introduction as he ate lunch. "The Bellefeuille Cruches represent a unique aspect of Cruche's vision," he composed, heartily enjoying fresh crab soufflé. "Not nearly enough has been said about Cruche and the nude."

The Senator broke in, asking how much Cruche was likely to fetch after the retrospective. Speck gave figures to which his choice of socks and cufflinks lent authority.

"Cruche-and-the-nude implies a definition of Woman," Speck continued, silently, sipping coffee from a gold-rimmed cup. "Lilith, Eve, temptress, saint, child, mother, nurse— Cruche delineated the feminine factor once and for all."

The Senator saw his guest to the door, took his briefcase from the hands of a manservant, and bestowed it on Speck like a diploma. He told Speck he would send him a personal invitation list for the Cruche opening next May. The list would include the estranged wife of a respected royal pretender, the publisher of an influential morning paper, the president of a nationalized bank, and the highest-ranking administrative official of a thickly populated area. Before driving away, Speck took a deep breath of west-end air. It was cool and dry, like Speck's new expression.

That evening, around closing time, he called Lydia Cruche. He had to let her know that the show could go on without her. "I shall be showing the Bellefeuille Cruches," he said.

"The *what*?"

Speck changed the subject. "There is enormous American interest," he said, meaning that he had written half a dozen letters and received prudent answers or none at all. He was accustomed to the tense excitement "American interest" could arouse. He had known artists to enroll in crash courses at Berlitz, the better to understand prices quoted in English.

Lydia was silent; then she said, slowly, "Don't ever mention such a thing again. Hube was anti-American—especially during the war." As for Lydia, she had set foot in the United States once, when a marshmallow roast had taken her a few yards inside North Dakota, some sixty years before.

The time was between half past seven and eight. Walter had gone to early dinner and a lecture on lost Atlantis. The Belgian painter was back in Bruges, unsold and unsung. The cultural-affairs committee had turned Speck's bill for expenses over to a law firm in Brussels. Two Paris galleries had folded in the past month and a third was packing up for America, where Speck gave it less than a year. Painters set adrift by these frightening changes drifted to other galleries, shipwrecked victims trying to crawl on board waterlogged rafts. On all sides Speck heard that the economic decline was irreversible. He knew one thing—art had sunk low on the scale of consumer necessities. To mop up a few back bills, he was showing part of his own collection—his last-ditch old-age-security reserve. He clasped his hands behind his neck, staring at a Vlaminck India ink on his desk. It had been certified genuine by an expert now serving a jail sentence in Zurich. Speck was planning to flog it to one of the ambassadors down the street.

He got up and began turning out lights, leaving just a spot in the window. To have been anti-American during the Second World War in France had a strict political meaning. Any hope of letters from Louis Aragon and Elsa withered and died: Hubert Cruche had been far Right. Of course, there was Right and Right, thought Speck as he triple-locked the front door. Nowadays the Paris intelligentsia drew new lines across the past, separating coarse collaborators from fine-drawn intellectual Fascists. One could no longer lump together young hotheads whose passionate belief in Europe had led them straight to the Charlemagne Division of the Waffen-S.S. and the soft middle class that had stayed behind to make money on the black market. Speck could not quite remember why *pure* Fascism had been better for civilization than the other kind, but somewhere on the safe side of the barrier there was bound to be a slot for Cruche. From the street, he considered a page of Charles Despiau sketches—a woman's hand, her breast, her thigh. He thought of the Senator's description of that other, early Lydia and of the fragments of perfection Speck could now believe in, for he had seen the Bellefeuille nudes. The familiar evening sadness caught up with him and lodged in his heart. Posterity forgives, he repeated, turning away, crossing the road on his way to his dinner.

Speck's ritual pause brought him up to St. Amand and his demon just as M. Chassepoule leaned into his window to replace a two-volume work he had probably taken out to show a customer. The bookseller drew himself straight, stared confidently into the night, and caught sight of Speck. The two greeted each other through glass. M. Chassepoule seemed safe, at ease, tucked away in a warm setting of lights and friends and royal blue, and yet he made an odd little gesture of helplessness, as if to tell Speck, "Here I am, like you, overtaxed, hounded, running an honest business against dreadful odds." Speck made a wry face of sympathy, as if to answer that he knew, he knew. His neighbor seemed to belong to an old and desperate breed, its back to the wall, its birthright gnawed away by foreigners, by the heathen, by the blithe continuity of art, by Speck himself. He dropped his gaze, genuinely troubled, examining the wares M. Chassepoule had collected, dusted, sorted, and priced for a new and ardent generation. The work he had just put back in the window was *La France Juive*, by Édouard Drumont. A handwritten notice described it as a classic study, out of print, hard to find, and in good condition.

Speck thought, A few years ago, no one would have dared put it on display. It has been considered rubbish for fifty years. Édouard Drumont died poor, alone, cast off even by his old friends, completely discredited. Perhaps his work was always being sold, quietly, somewhere, and I didn't know. Had he been Walter and superstitious, he might have crossed his fingers; being Speck and rational, he merely shuddered.

Walter had a friend—Félicité Blum-Weiler-Bloch, the owner of the Afghan hound. When Walter complained to her about the temperature of the gallery, she gave him a scarf, a sweater, an old flannel bed-sheet, and a Turkey carpet. Walter decided to make a present of the carpet to Speck.

"Get that thing out of my gallery," said Speck.

"It's really from Félicité."

"I don't want her here, either," said Speck. "Or the dog."

Walter proposed spreading the carpet on the floor in the basement. "I spend a lot of time there," he said. "My feet get cold."

"I want it out," said Speck.

Later that day Speck discovered Walter down in the framing room, holding a vacuum cleaner. The Turkey carpet was spread on the floor. A stripe of neutral color ran through the pattern of mottled reds and blues. Looking closer, Speck saw it was warp and weft. "Watch," said Walter. He switched on the vacuum; another strip of color vanished. "The wool lifts right out," said Walter.

"I told you to get rid of it," said Speck, trembling.

"Why? I can still use it."

"I won't have my gallery stuffed with filth."

"You'll never have to see it. You hardly ever come down here." He ran the vacuum, drowning Speck's reply. Over the noise Walter yelled, "It will look better when it's all one color."

Speck raised his voice to the Right Wing pitch heard during street fights: "Get it out! Get it out of my gallery!"

Like a telephone breaking into a nightmare, delivering the sleeper, someone was calling, "Dr. Speck." There on the stairs stood Lydia Cruche, wearing an ankle-length fur coat and a brown velvet turban. "I thought I'd better have a look at the place," she said. "Just to see how much space you have, how much of Cruche you can hold."

Still trembling, Speck took her hand, which smelled as if she had been peeling oranges, and pressed it to his lips.

That evening, Speck called the Senator: Would he be interested in writing the catalogue introduction? No one was better fitted, said Speck, over senatorial modesty. The Senator had kept faith with Cruche. During his years of disappointment and eclipse Cruche had been heartened, knowing that guests at the Senator's table could lift their eyes from quail in aspic to feast on "Nude in the Afternoon."

Perhaps his lodge brother exaggerated just a trifle, the Senator replied, though it was true that he had hung on to his Cruches even when their value had been wiped out of the market. The only trouble was that his recent prose had been about the capital-gains-tax project, the Common Market sugar-beet subsidy, and the uninformed ecological campaign against plastic containers. He wondered if he could write with the same persuasiveness about art.

"I have taken the liberty of drawing up an outline," said Speck. "Just a few notes. Knowing how busy you are."

Hanging up, he glanced at his desk calendar. Less than six weeks had gone by since the night when, by moonlight, Speck had heard the Senator saying ". . . hats."

A few days before Christmas Speck drove out to Lydia's with a briefcase filled with documents that were, at last, working papers: the list of exhibits from the Bellefeuille collection, the introduction, and the chronology in which there were gaps for Lydia to fill. He still had to draw up a financial arrangement. So far, she had said nothing about it, and it was not a matter Speck cared to rush.

He found another guest in the house—a man somewhat younger than he, slightly bald and as neat as a mouse.

"Here's the doctor I was telling you about," said Lydia, introducing Speck.

Signor Vigorelli of Milan was a fellow-Japhethite—so Speck gathered from their conversation, which took up, in English, as though he had never come in. Lydia poured Speck's tea in an offhand manner he found wounding. He felt he was being treated like the hanger-on in a Russian play. He smashed his lemon cupcake, scattering crumbs. The visitor's plate looked cleaner than his. After a minute of this, Speck took the catalogue material out of his briefcase and started to read. Nobody asked what he was reading. The Italian finally looked at his watch (expensive, of a make Speck recognized) and got to his feet, picking up car keys that had been lying next to his plate.

"That little man had an Alfa Romeo tag," said Speck when Lydia returned after seeing him out.

"I don't know why you people drive here when there is perfectly good bus service," she said.

"What does he do?"

"He is a devout, religious man."

For the first time, she sat down on the sofa, close to Speck. He showed her the introduction and the chronology. She made a number of sharp and useful suggestions. Then they went upstairs and looked at the pictures. The studio had been cleaned, the light repaired. Speck suddenly thought, I've done it—I've brought it off.

"We must discuss terms," he said.

"When you're ready," she replied. "Your cold seems a lot better."

Inching along in stagnant traffic, Speck tried one after the other the FM state-controlled stations on his car radio. He obtained a lecture about the cultural oppression of Cajuns in Louisiana, a warning that the road he was now driving on was saturated, and the disheartening squeaks and wails of a circumcision ceremony in Ethiopia. On the station called France-Culture someone said, "Henri Cruche."

"Not Henri, excuse me," said a polite foreigner. "His name was Hubert. Hubert Cruche."

"Strange that it should be an Italian to discover an artist so essentially French," said the interviewer.

Signor Vigorelli explained that his admiration for France was second only to his intense feelings about Europe. His career had been consecrated to enhancing Italian elegance with French refinement and then scattering the result abroad. He believed that the unjustly neglected Cruche would be a revelation and might even bring the whole of Western art to its senses.

Speck nodded, agreeing. The interview came to an end. Wild jungle drums broke forth, heralding the announcement that there was to be a reading of medieval Bulgarian poetry in an abandoned factory at Nanterre. It was then and then only that Speck took in the sense of what he had heard. He swung the car in a wild U-turn and, without killing himself or anyone else, ran into a tree. He sat quietly, for about a minute, until his breathing became steady again, then unlocked his safety belt and got out. For a long time he stood by the side of the road, holding his briefcase, feeling neither shock nor pain. Other drivers, noticing a man alone with a wrecked car, picked up speed. He began to walk in Lydia's direction. A cruising prostitute, on her way home to cook her husband's dinner, finally agreed to drop him off at a taxi stand. Speck gave her two hundred francs.

Lydia did not seem at all surprised to see him. "I'd invite you to supper," she said. "But all I've got is a tiny pizza and some of the leftover cake."

"The Italian," said Speck.

"Yes?"

"I've heard him. On the radio. He says he's got Cruche. That he discovered him. My car is piled up in the Bois. I tried to turn around and come back here. I've been walking for hours."

"Sit down," said Lydia. "There, on the sofa. Signor Vigorelli is having a big Cruche show in Milan next March."

"He can't," said Speck.

"Why can't he?"

"Because Cruche is mine. He was my idea. No one can have my idea. Not until after June."

"Then it goes to Trieste in April," said Lydia. "You could still have it by about the tenth of May. If you still want it."

If I want it, said Speck to himself. If I want it. With the best work sold and the insurance rates tripled and the commissions shared out like candy. And with everyone saying Speck jumped on the bandwagon, Speck made the last train.

"Lydia, listen to me," he said. "I invented Hubert Cruche. There would be no Hubert Cruche without Sandor Speck. This is an unspeakable betrayal. It is dishonorable. It is wrong." She listened, nodding her head. "What happens to me now?" he said. "Have you thought about that?" He knew better than to ask, "Why didn't you tell me about him?" Like all dissembling women, she would simply answer, "Tell you what?"

"It might be all the better," she said. "There'll be that much more interest in Hube."

"Interest?" said Speck. "The worst kind of interest. Third-rate, tawdry interest. Do you suppose I can get the Pompidou Center to look at a painter who has been trailing around in Trieste? It had to be a new idea. It had to be strong."

"You'll save on the catalogue," she said. "He will probably want to share."

"It's my catalogue," said Speck. "I'm not sharing. Senator Bellefeuille...my biography...never. The catalogue is mine. Besides, it would look as if he'd had the idea."

"He did."

"But after me," said Speck, falling back on the most useless of all lover's arguments. "*After* me. I was there first."

"So you were," she said tenderly, like any woman on her way out.

Speck said, "I thought you were happy with our arrangement."

"I was. But I hadn't met him yet. You see, he was so interested in the Japhethite movement. One day he opened the Bible and put his finger on something that seemed to make it all right about the graven image. In Ecclesiastes, I think."

Speck gave up. "I suppose it would be no use calling for a taxi?"

"Not around here, I'm afraid, though you might pick one up at the shopping center. Shouldn't you report the accident?"

"Which accident?"

"To the police," she said. "Get it on record fast. Make it a case. That squeezes the insurance people. The phone's in the hall."

"I don't care about the insurance," said Speck.

"You will care, once you're over the shock. Tell me exactly where it happened. Can you remember? Have you got your license? Registration? Insurance?"

Speck sank back and closed his eyes. He could hear Lydia dialling; then she began to speak. He listened, exactly as Cruche must have listened, while Lydia, her voice full of silver bells, dealt with creditors and dealers and Cruche's castoff girlfriends and a Senator Bellefeuille more than forty years younger.

"I wish to report an accident," Lydia sang. "The victim is Dr. S. Speck. He is still alive—luckily. He was forced off the road in the Bois de Vincennes by a tank truck carrying high-octane fuel. It had an Italian plate. Dr. Speck was too shaken to get the number. Yes, I saw the accident, but I couldn't see the number. There was a van in the way. All I noticed was 'MI.' That must stand for Milan. I recognized the victim. Dr. Speck is well known in some circles...an intimate friend of Senator Antoine Bellefeuille, the former Minister of...that's right." She talked a few minutes longer, then came back to Speck. "Get in touch with the insurance people first thing tomorrow," she said, flat Lydia again. "Get a medical certificate—you've had a serious emotional trauma. It can lead to jaundice. Tell your doctor to write that down. If he doesn't want to, I'll give you the name of a doctor who will. You're on the edge of nervous depression. By the way, the police will be towing your car to a garage. They know they've been very remiss, letting a foreign vehicle with a dangerous cargo race through the Bois. It might have hit a bus full of children. They must be looking for that tanker all over Paris. I've made a list of the numbers you're to call."

Speck produced his last card: "Senator Bellefeuille will never allow his Cruches to go to Milan. He'll never let them out of the country."

"Who—Antoine?" said Lydia. "Of course he will."

She cut a cupcake in half and gave him a piece. Broken, Speck crammed the whole thing in his mouth. She stood over him, humming. "Do you know that old hymn, Dr. Speck—'The day Thou gavest, Lord, is ended'?"

He searched her face, as he had often, looking for irony, or playfulness—a gleam of light. There floated between them the cold oblong on the map and the Chirico chessboard moving along to its Arctic destination. Trees dwindled to shrubs and shrubs to moss and moss to nothing. Speck had been defeated by a landscape.

Although Speck by no means considered himself a natural victim of hard luck, he had known disappointment. Shows had fallen flat. Galleries had been blown up and torn down. Artists he had nursed along had been lured away by siren dealers. Women had wandered off, bequeathing to Speck the warp and weft of a clear situation, so much less interesting than the ambiguous patterns of love. Disappointment had taught him rules: the first was that it takes next to no time to get used to bad news. Rain began to fall as he walked to the taxi stand. In his mind, Cruche was already being shown in Milan and he was making the best of it.

He gazed up and down the bleak road; of course there were no taxis. Inside a bus shelter huddled a few commuters. The thrust of their lives, their genetic destiny obliged them to wait for public transport—unlike Speck, thrown among them by random adventures. A plastic-covered timetable announced a bus to Paris every twenty-three minutes until five, every sixteen minutes from four to eight, and every thirty-one minutes thereafter. His watch had stopped late in the afternoon, probably at the time of the accident. He left the shelter and stood out in the wet, looking at windows of shops, one of which might contain a clock. He stood for a minute or two staring at a china tea set flanked by two notices: "Hand Painted" and "Christmas Is Coming," both of which he found deeply sad. The tea set had been decorated with reproductions of the Pompidou Art Center, which was gradually replacing the Eiffel Tower as a constituent feature of French design. The day's shocks caught up with him: he stared at the milk jug, feeling surprise because it did not tell him the time. The arrival of a bus replaced this perplexity with one more pressing. He did not know what was needed on suburban buses—tickets or tokens or a monthly pass. He wondered whether the drivers accepted banknotes, and gave change, with civility.

"Dr. Speck, Dr. Speck!" Lydia Cruche, her raincoat open and flying, waving a battered black umbrella, bore down on him out of the dark. "You were right," she said, gasping. "You were there first." Speck took his place at the end of the bus queue. "I mean it," she said, clutching his arm. "He can wait."

Speck's second rule of disappointment came into play: the deceitful one will always come back to you ten seconds too late. "What does it mean?" he said, wiping rain from the end of his nose. "Having it before him means what? Paying for the primary expenses and the catalogue and sweetening the Paris critics and letting him rake in the chips?"

"Wasn't that what you wanted?"

"Your chap from Milan thought he was first," said Speck. "He may not want to step aside for me—a humble Parisian expert on the entire Cruche context and period. You wouldn't want Cruche to miss a chance at Milan, either."

"Milan is ten times better for money than Paris," she said. "If that's what we're talking about. But of course we aren't."

Speck looked down at her from the step of the bus. "Very well," he said. "As we were."

"I'll come to the gallery," she called. "I'll be there tomorrow. We can work out new terms."

Speck paid his fare without trouble and moved to the far end of the bus. The dark shopping center with its windows shining for no one was a Magritte vision of fear. Lydia had already forgotten him. Having tampered with his pride, made a professional ass of him, gone off with his idea and returned it dented and chipped, she now stood gazing at the Pompidou Center tea set, perhaps wondering if the ban on graven images could possibly extend to this. Speck had often meant to ask her about the Mickey Mouse napkins. He thought of the hoops she had put him through— God, and politics, and finally the most dangerous one, which was jealousy. There seemed to be no way of rolling down the window, but a sliding panel at the top admitted half his face. Rising from his seat, he drew in a gulp of wet suburban air and threw it out as a shout: "Fascist! Fascist! Fascist!"

Not a soul in the bus turned to see. From the look of them, they had spent the best Sundays of their lives shuffling in demonstrations from Place de la République to Place de la Nation, tossing "Fascist"'s around like confetti. Lydia turned slowly and looked at Speck. She raised her umbrella at arm's length, like a trophy. For the first time, Speck saw her smile. What was it the Senator had said? "She had a smile like a fox's." He could see, gleaming white, her straight little animal teeth.

The bus lurched away from the curb and lumbered toward Paris. Speck leaned back and shut his eyes. Now he understood about that parting shot. It was amazing how it cleared the mind, tearing out weeds and tree stumps, flattening the live stuff along with the dead. "Fascist" advanced like a regiment of tanks. Only the future remained—clean, raked, ready for new growth. New growth of what? Of Cruche, of course—Cruche, whose hour was at hand, whose time was here. Speck began to explore his altered prospects. "New terms," she had said. So far, there had been none at all. The sorcerer from Milan must have promised something dazzling, swinging it before her eyes as he had swung his Alfa Romeo key. It would be foolish to match the offer. By the time they had all done with bungling, there might not be enough left over to buy a new Turkey carpet for Walter.

I was no match for her, he thought. No match at all. But then, look at the help she had—that visitation from Cruche. "Only once," she said, but women always said that: "He asked if he could see me just once more. I couldn't very well refuse." Dead or alive, when it came to confusion and double-dealing, there was no such thing as "only once." And there had been not only the departed Cruche but the very living Senator Bellefeuille— "Antoine"; who had bought every picture of Lydia for sixteen years, the span of her early beauty. Nothing would ever be the same again between Speck and Lydia, of course. No man could give the same trust and confidence the second time around. All that remained to them was the patch of landscape they held in common—a domain reserved for the winning, collecting, and sharing out of profits, a territory where believer and skeptic, dupe and embezzler, the loving and the faithless could walk hand in hand. Lydia had a talent for money. He could sense it. She had never been given much chance to use it, and she had waited so much longer than Speck.

He opened his eyes and saw rain clouds over Paris glowing with light—the urban aurora. It seemed to Speck that he was entering a better weather zone, leaving behind the gray, indefinite mist in which the souls of discarded lovers are said to wander. He welcomed this new and brassy radiation. He saw himself at the center of a shadeless drawing, hero of a sort of cartoon strip, subduing Lydia, taming Henriette. Fortunately, he was above petty grudges. Lydia and Henriette had been designed by a bachelor God who had let the creation get out of hand. In the cleared land of Speck's future, a yellow notebook fluttered and lay open at a new page. The show would be likely to go to Milan in the autumn now; it might be a good idea to slip a note between the Senator's piece and the biographical chronology. If Cruche had to travel, then let it be with Speck's authority as his passport.

The bus had reached its terminus, the city limit. Speck waited as the rest of the passengers crept inch by inch to the doors. He saw, with immense relief, a rank of taxis half a block long. He alighted and strode toward them, suddenly buoyant. He seemed to have passed a mysterious series of tests, and to have been admitted to some new society, the purpose of which he did not yet understand. He was a saner, stronger, wiser person than the Sandor Speck who had seen his own tight smile on M. Chassepoule's window only two months before. As he started to get into a taxi, a young man darted toward him and thrust a leaflet into his hand. Speck shut the door, gave his address, and glanced at the flyer he was still holding. Crudely printed on cheap pink paper was this:

FRENCHMEN!
FOR THE SAKE OF EUROPE, FIGHT
THE GERMANO-AMERICANO-ISRAELO
HEGEMONY!
Germans in Germany!
Americans in America!
Jews in Israel!
For a True Europe, For One Europe,
Death to the Anti-European Hegemony!

Speck stared at this without comprehending it. Was it a Chassepoule statement or an anti-Chassepoule plea? There was no way of knowing. He turned it over, looking for the name of an association, and immediately forgot what he was seeking. Holding the sheet of paper flat on his briefcase, he began to write, as well as the unsteady swaying of the cab would let him.

"It was with instinctive prescience that Hubert Cruche saw the need for a Europe united from the Atlantic to the...That Cruche skirted the murky zone of partisan politics is a tribute to his...even though his innocent zeal may have led him to the brink...early meeting with the young idealist and future statesman A. Bellefeuille, whose penetrating essay...close collaboration with the artist's wife and most trusted critic...and now, posthumously...from Paris, where the retrospective was planned and brought to fruition by the undersigned...and on to Italy, to the very borders of..."

Because this one I am keeping, Speck decided; this one will be signed: "By Sandor Speck." He smiled at the bright, wet streets of Paris as he and Cruche, together, triumphantly crossed the Alps.

OVERHEAD IN A BALLOON

Aymeric had a family name that Walter at first didn't catch. He had come into the art gallery as "A. Régis," which was how he signed his work. He must have been close to sixty, but only his self-confidence had kept pace with time. His eyes shone, young and expectant, in an unlined and rosy face. In spite of the face, almost downy, he was powerful-looking, with a wrestler's thrust of neck and hunched shoulders. Walter, assistant manager of the gallery, was immediately attracted to Aymeric, as to a new religion—this time, one that might work.

Painting portraits on commission had seen Aymeric through the sunnier decades, but there were fewer clients now, at least in Europe. After a brief late flowering of Moroccan princes and Pakistani generals, he had given up. Now he painted country houses. Usually he showed the front with the white shutters and all the ivy, and a stretch of lawn with white chairs and a teapot and cups, and some scattered pages of *Le Figaro*—the only newspaper, often the only anything, his patrons read. He had a hairline touch and could reproduce *Le Figaro*'s social calendar, in which he cleverly embedded his client's name and his own.

Some patrons kept a large magnifying glass on a table under the picture, so that guests, peering respectfully, could appreciate their host's permanent place in art.

Unfortunately, such commissions never amounted to much. These were not the great homes of France (they had all been done long ago, and in times of uncertainty and anxious thrift the heirs and owners were not of a mind to start over) but weekend places. Aymeric was called in to immortalize a done-up village bakery, a barn refurbished and brightened with the yellow awnings "Dallas" had lately made so popular. They were not houses meant to be handed on but slabs of Paris-area real estate, to be sold and sold again, each time with a thicker garnish of improvements. Aymeric had by now worked his territory to the farthest limit of the farthest flagged terrace within a two-hour drive from Paris in any direction; it had occurred to him that a show, a sort of retrospective of lawns and *Figaros*, would bring fresh patronage, perhaps even from abroad. (As Walter was to discover, Aymeric was blankly unprofessional, with that ignorance of the trade peculiar to its fringe.) It happened that one of the Paris Sunday supplements had published a picture story on Walter's gallery, with captions that laid stress on the establishment's boldness, vitality, visibility, international connections, and financial vigor. The supplement project had cost Walter's employer a packet, and Walter was not surprised that one of the photographs showed him close to collapse, leaning for support against the wall safe in his private office. The accompanying article described mobbed openings, private viewings to which the police were summoned to keep order, and potential buyers lined up outside in below-freezing weather, bursting in the minute the doors were opened to grab everything off the walls. The name of the painter hardly mattered; the gallery's reputation was enough.

Who believes this, Walter had wondered, turning the slippery, rainbow pages. Then Aymeric had lumbered in, pink and hopeful, believing.

He had dealt with, and been dealt with by, Walter's employer, known privately to Walter as "Trout Face." Aymeric showed courteous amazement when he heard just how much a show of that kind would cost. The uncultured talk about money was the gallery's way of refusing him, though a clause in the rejection seemed to say that something might still be feasible, in some distant off-season, provided that Aymeric was willing to buy all his own work. He declined, politely. For that matter, Trout Face was civil, too.

Walter, from behind his employer's back, had been letting Aymeric know by means of winks and signs that he might be able to help. (In the end, he was no help.) He managed to make an appointment to meet Aymeric in a café not far away, on Boulevard Saint-Germain. There, a few hours later, they sat on the glass-walled sidewalk terrace—it was March, and still cold—with Walter suddenly feeling Swiss and insufficient as Aymeric delicately unfolded a long banner of a name. Walter had already introduced himself, much more briefly: "Obermauer." He pointed, because the conversation could not get going again, and said, "That's my Métro station, over there. Solférino."

They had been through some of Aymeric's troubles and were sliding, Walter hoped, along to his own. These were, in order, that for nine years his employer had been exploiting him; that he had a foot caught in the steel teeth of his native Calvinism and was hoping to ease it free without resorting to a knife; that the awfully nice Dominican who had been lending books to him had brusquely advised him to try psychoanalysis. Finally, the apartment building he lived in had just been sold to a chain of health clubs, and everybody had to get out. It seemed a great deal to set loose on a new friend, so Walter mentioned only that he had a long underground ride to work every day, with two changes.

Aymeric replied that from the Notre-Dame-des-Champs station there was no change. That was how he had come, lugging his portfolio to show Walter's employer. "I was too soft with him, probably," Aymeric resumed. His relatives had already turned out to be his favorite topic. "The men in my family are too tolerant. Our wives leave us for brutes."

Leaning forward the better to hear Aymeric, who had dropped to a mutter, Walter noticed that his hair was dyed, pale locks on a ruddy forehead. His voice ran like clockwork, drawling to a stop and then, wound up tight, picking up again, like a refreshed countertenor. His voice was like the signature that required a magnifying glass; what he had to say was clear, but a kind of secret.

Walter said he was astonished at the number of men willing to admit, with no false pride, that their wives had left them.

"Oh, well, they do that nowadays," said Aymeric. "They wait for the children to." To? He must have meant "to grow up, to leave home."

"Are there children?" He imagined Aymeric lingering outside the fence of a schoolyard, trying to catch a glimpse of his estranged children, ducking behind a parked car when a teacher looked his way.

"Grandchildren."

Walter continued to feel sympathy. His employer, back in the days when he had been training Walter to be a gallery instrument as silent and reliable as the lock on the office safe, had repeatedly warned him that wives were death to the art trade. Degas had remained a bachelor. Did Walter know why? Because Degas did not want to have a wife looking at his work at the end of the day and remarking, "That's pretty."

They had finally got the conversation rolling evenly. Aymeric, wound up and in good breath, revealed that he and his cousin Robert and Robert's aged mother occupied a house his family had lived in forever. Actually, it was on one floor of an apartment building, but nearly the whole story—three sides of the court. For a long time, it had been a place the women of the family could come back to when their husbands died or began showing the indifference that amounts to desertion. Now that Paris had changed so much, it was often the men who returned. (Walter noticed that Aymeric said "Paris" instead of "life," or "manners," or "people.") Probably laziness of habit had made him say they had lived forever between the Luxembourg Gardens and the Boulevard Raspail. Raspail was less than a century old, and could scarcely count as a timeless landmark. Still, when Aymeric looked down at the damp cobblestones in the court, out of his kitchen window, he could not help feeling behind him the line of ancestors who had looked out, too, wondering, like Aymeric, if it really would be a mortal sin to jump.

Robert, his cousin, owned much of the space. It was space one carved up, doled out anew, remodelled; it was space on which one was taxed. Sixty square metres had just been sold to keep the city of Paris from grabbing twice that amount for back taxes. Another piece had gone to pay their share in mending the roof. Over the years, as so many single, forsaken adults had tried to construct something nestlike, cushioning, clusters of small living quarters had evolved, almost naturally, like clusters of coral. All the apartments connected; one could walk from end to end of the floor without having to step out to a landing. They never locked their doors. Members of the same family do not steal from one another, and they have nothing to hide. Aymeric said this almost sternly. Robert's wife had died, he added, just as Walter opened his mouth to ask. Death was the same thing as desertion.

Walter did not know what to answer to all this, especially to the part about locks. A good, stout bolt seemed to him a sensible and not an unfriendly precaution. "And lead us not into temptation," he was minded to quote, but it was too soon to begin that ambiguous sort of exchange.

At that moment Walter's employer appeared across the boulevard, at the curb, trying to flag a taxi by waving his briefcase. None stopped, and he moved away, perhaps to a bus stop. Walter wondered where he was going, then remembered that he didn't care.

"I hate him," he told Aymeric. "I *hate* him. I dream he is in danger. A patrol car drives up and the execution squad takes him away. I dream he is drinking coffee after dinner and far off in the night you can hear the patrol car, coming to get him."

Aymeric wondered what bound Walter to that particular dealer. There were other employers in Paris, just as dedicated to art.

"I hate art, too," said Walter. "Oh, I don't mean that I hate what you do. That, at least, has some meaning—it lets people see how they imagine they live."

Aymeric's tongue rested on his lower lip as he considered this. Walter explained that he had to spend another eleven years working for Trout Face if he was to get the full benefit of a twenty-year pension fund. In eleven years, he would be forty-six. He hoped there was still enjoyment to be had at that age.

"When you are drawing retirement pay, I'll be working for a living," Aymeric said. He let his strong, elderly hands rest on the table—evidence, of a kind.

"At first, when I thought I could pull my funds out at any time, I used to give notice," Walter went on. "When I stopped giving notice, he turned mean. I dreamed last night that there was a bomb under the floor of the gallery. He nearly blew himself up digging it out. He was saved. He is always saved. He escapes, or the thing doesn't explode, or the chief of the execution squad changes his mind."

"Robert has a book about dreams," said Aymeric. "He can look it up. I want him to meet you."

About four weeks after this, Walter moved into two rooms, kitchen, and bathroom standing empty between Robert's quarters and his mother's. It was Robert who looked after the practical side of the household and to whom Walter paid a surprisingly hefty rent; but he was on a direct Métro line, and within reach of friendship, and, for the first time since he had left Bern to work in Paris, he felt close to France.

That spring Robert's mother had grown old. She could not always remember where she was, or the age of her two children. At night she roamed about, turning on lights, opening bedroom doors. (Walter, who felt no responsibility toward her, kept his locked.) She picked up curios and trinkets and left them anywhere. Once a month Robert and Aymeric traded back paperweights and snuffboxes.

One night she entered her son's bedroom at two in the morning, pulled open a drawer, and began throwing his shirts on the floor. She was packing to send him on a summer holiday. Halfway through (her son pretended to be asleep), she turned her mind to Aymeric. Aymeric woke up a few minutes later to find his aunt in bed beside him, with her finger in her mouth. He got up and spent the rest of the night in an armchair.

"Why don't you knock her out with pills?" Walter asked him.

"We can't do that. It might kill her."

What's the difference, said Walter's face. "Then shut her up in her own bedroom."

"She might not like that. By the way, here's your phone bill."

Walter was surprised at the abruptness of the deadlock. Aymeric did not so much change the subject as tear it up. Walter could not understand many things—the amount of his telephone bill, for instance. He did most of his calling from the gallery, dialling his parents in Bern with the warm feeling that he was putting one over on Trout Face. He had been astonished to learn that he was supposed to pay a monthly fee for using the elevator. Apparently, it was the custom of the house. Aymeric was turning out to be less of a new religion than Walter had expected. For one thing, he was seldom there. His old life moved on, in an unseen direction, and he did not offer to bring Walter along. He seemed idle yet at the same time busy. He hardly ever sat down without giving the impression that he was trying to get to his feet; barely entered a room without starting to edge his way out of it. Running his fingers through his pale, abundant hair, he said, "I've got an awful lot to do."

Reading in bed one night, Walter glanced up and had the eerie sight of a doorknob silently turning. "Let me in," Robert's mother called. Her voice was sweet and pitched to childhood. "The latch is caught, and I can't use both hands." Walter tied the sash of the Old England dressing gown his employer had given him one Christmas, when they were still getting along.

She had put on lipstick and eye-shadow. "I'm taking my children to Mass," she said, "and I thought I'd just leave this with you." She opened her fist, clenched like a baby's, and offered Walter a round gold snuffbox with a cameo portrait on its lid. He set the box down on a marble-topped table and led her through a labyrinth of low-ceilinged rooms to Robert's bedroom door, where he left her. She went straight in, turning on an overhead light.

By morning, the box had drawn in the cold of the marble, but it became warm in Walter's hand. He and his employer were barely speaking; they often used sign language to show that something had to be moved or hung up or taken down. Walter seemed to be trying to play a guessing game until he opened his hand, as Robert's mother had done.

"Just something I picked up," he said, as if he had been combing second-hand junk stores and was no fool.

"Picked up where?" said his employer, appreciating the weight and feel of the gold. He changed his spectacles for a stronger pair, ran his thumb lightly and affectionately over the cameo. "Messalina," he said. "Look at those curls." He held the box at eye level, tipping it slightly, and said, "Glued on. An amateur job. Where did you say you got it?"

"I happened to pick it up."

"Well, you'd better put it back." A bright spot moved on his bald head as he leaned into the light. "Or, wait; leave it. I'll look at it again." He wrapped the box in a paper handkerchief and locked it up in his safe.

"I brought it just to show you," said Walter.

His employer motioned as if he were pushing a curtain aside with the back of his right hand. It meant, Go away.

Robert was in charge of a small laboratory on the Rue de Vaugirard. He sat counting blood cells in a basement room. Walter imagined Robert pushing cells along the wire of an abacus, counting them off by ten. (He was gently discouraged from paying a visit. Robert explained there was no extra chair.) In the laboratory they drew and analyzed blood samples. Patients came in with their doctor's instructions, Social Security number, often a thick file of medical history they tried to get Robert to read, and blood was taken from a vein in the crook of the arm. The specimen had to be drawn before breakfast; even a cup of coffee could spoil the result. Sometimes patients fainted and were late for appointments. Robert revived them with red wine.

Each morning, Robert put on a track suit and ran in the Luxembourg Gardens, adroitly slipping past runners whose training program had them going the other way. Many of the neighborhood shopkeepers ran. The greengrocer and the Spaniard from the hardware store signalled greetings with their eyes. It was not etiquette to stop and talk, and they had to save breath.

Walter admired Robert's thinness, his clean running shoes, his close-cropped gray hair. When he was not running, he seemed becalmed. He could sit listening to Walter as if he were drifting and there was nothing but Walter in sight. Walter told him about his employer, and the nice Dominican, and how both, in their different spheres, had proved disappointing. He refrained from mentioning Aymeric, whose friendship had so quickly fallen short of Walter's. He did not need to be psychoanalyzed, he said. No analysis could resolve his wish to attain the Church of Rome, or remove the Protestant martyrs who stood barring the way.

Sometimes Robert made a controlled and quiet movement while Walter was speaking, such as moving a clean silver ashtray an inch. No one was allowed to smoke in his rooms, but they were furnished with whatever one might require. Walter confessed that he admired everything French, even the ashtrays, and Robert nodded his head, as if to say that for an outsider it was bound to be so.

Robert got up at five and cleaned his rooms. (Aymeric had

someone who came in twice a week.) He ran, then came back to
change and eat a light breakfast before going to work. The first
thing he did at five was to put on a record of Mozart's Concerto
in C Major for Flute and Harp. He opened his windows;
everyone except Walter-the-Swiss slept with them tight shut.
The Allegro moved in a spiral around the courtyard, climbed
above the mended roof, and became thin and celestial.

Walter usually woke up in the middle of the Andantino. It was
much too early to get up. He turned on his side, away from the
day. The mysterious sadness he felt on waking he had until now
blamed on remoteness from God. Now he was beginning to
suppose that people really must be made in His image, for their
true face was just as concealed and their true whereabouts as
obscure. A long, dangerous trapeze swoop of friendship had
borne him from Aymeric's to Robert's side of the void, but all
Robert had done was make room for Walter on the platform. He
was accommodating, nothing more. Walter knew that he was too
old at thirty-five for those giddy, hopeful swings. One of these
days he was going to lose momentum and be left dangling,
without a safety net.

He could hear music, a vacuum cleaner, and sparrows. The
nice Dominican had assured him that God would still be there
when his analysis had run its course. From his employer he had
learned that sadness was supposed to be borne with every
outward sign of elegance. Walter had no idea what that was
supposed to mean. It meant nothing.

By the Rondo Allegro, Robert's mother would begin shaking
Aymeric awake. Aymeric guided her back to her own apartment
and began to boil water and grind coffee for her breakfast. She
always asked him what he was doing in her private quarters, and
where he had put his wife. She owned a scratched record of
"Luna Rossa" sung by Tino Rossi, to which she could listen
twelve times running without losing interest. It was a record of
the old, breakable kind, and Walter wondered why someone
didn't crack it on the edge of a sink. He thought of Farinelli, the

castrato who every evening for ten years had to sing the same four tunes to the King of Spain. Nothing had been written about the King's attendants—whether at the end of ten years there were any of them sane.

In his own kitchen, Aymeric brewed lime-flower tea. Later, an egg timer would let him know he was ready for coffee. If he drank coffee too soon, his digestive system became flooded with acid, which made him feel ill. Whenever Robert talked about redistributing the space, Aymeric would remark that he would be dead before long and they could do as they liked with his rooms. His roseate complexion concealed an ashen inner reality, he believed. Any qualified doctor looking at him saw at once that he was meant to be pale. He followed the tea with a bowl of bran (bought in a health-food store) soaked in warm water. After that, he was prepared for breakfast.

When Aymeric was paying a weekend visit to a new patron, in some remodelled village abattoir, he ate whatever they gave him. Artist-in-residence, he had no complaints. On the first evening, sipping a therapeutic Scotch (it lowered blood pressure and made arterial walls elastic), he would tactfully, gradually, drop his chain-link name: he was not only "A. Régis" but "Aymeric Something Something de Something de Saint-Régis." Like Picasso, he said, he had added his mother's maiden name. His hostess, rapidly changing her mind about dinner, would open a tin of foie gras and some bottled fruit from Fauchon's. On Monday, he would be driven home, brick-colored, his psychic image more ashen than ever. Rich food made him dream. He dreamed that someone had snubbed him. Sometimes it was the Archbishop of Paris, more often the Pope.

In a thick, thumbed volume he kept at his bedside, Robert looked up all their dreams. Employer, execution squad, patrol car, arrest combined to mean bright days ahead for someone especially dear to the dreamer. Animals denoted treachery. Walter, when not granted a vision of his employer's downfall, dreamed about dormice and moles. Treachery, Robert repeated,

closing the book. The harmless creatures were messengers of
betrayal.

Coming up from underground at the Chambre des Députés
station (his personal stop at Solférino was closed for repair)
one day, Walter looked around. On a soft May morning, this
most peaceful stretch of Boulevard Saint-Germain might be the
place where betrayal would strike. He crossed the road so that he
would not have to walk in front of the Ministry of Defense,
where men in uniform might make him say that his dreams about
patrol cars were seditious. After a block or so he crossed back and
made his way, with no further threats or dangers, to his place of
work.

Immersion in art had kept him from spiritual knowledge.
What he had mistaken for God's beckoning had been a dabbling
in colors, sentiment cut loose and set afloat by the sight of a
stained-glass window. Years before, when he was still training
Walter, his employer had sent him to museums, with a list of
things to examine and ponder. God is in art, Walter had decided;
then, God *is* art. Today, he understood: art is God's enemy. God
hates art, the trifling rival creation.

Aymeric, when Walter announced his revelation, closed his
eyes. Closing his eyes, he seemed to go deaf. It was odd, because
last March, in the café, he had surely been listening. Robert
listened. His blue gaze never wavered from a point just above
Walter's head. When Walter had finished, Robert said that as a
native Catholic he did not have to worry about God and art, or
God and anything. All the worrying had already been done for
him. Walter replied that no one had ever finished with worrying,
and he offered to lend Robert books.

Robert returned Walter's books unread. He was showing the
native Catholic resistance to religious history and theology. He
did not want to learn more about St. Augustine and St. Thomas
Aquinas than he had been told years before, in his private school.
Having had the great good luck to be born into the only true

faith, he saw no reason to rake the subject over. He did not go in for pounding his head on an open door. (Those were Robert's actual words.)

Robert's favorite topic was not God but the administration of the city of Paris, to which he felt bound by the ownership of so many square metres of urban space. He would look withdrawn and Gothic when anyone said, "The city does such a lot for the elderly now." The latest folderol was having old people taken up for helicopter rides, at taxpayers' expense. Robert's mother heard about the free rides while toying with a radio. Robert borrowed his sister's car and drove his mother to the helicopter field near the Porte de Versailles, where they found a group of pensioners waiting their turn. He was told he could not accompany his mother aloft: he was only forty-nine.

"I don't need anyone," his mother said. She unpinned her hat of beige straw and handed it to him. He watched strangers help her aboard, along with three other old women and a man with a limp. Robert raised his hands to his ears, hat and all, against the noise. His mother ascended rapidly. In less than twenty minutes she was back, making sure, before she would tell him about the trip, that he had not damaged her hat. The old gentleman had an arthritic leg, which he had stuck out at an awkward angle, inconveniencing one of the ladies. The pilot had spoken once, to say, "You can see Orléans." When the helicopter dipped, all the old hens screamed, she said. In her own mind, except now and then, she was about twenty-eight. She made Robert promise he would write a letter to the authorities, telling them there should be a cassette on board with a spoken travelogue and light music. She pulled on her hat, and in its lacy shadow resembled her old black-and-white snapshots, from the time before Robert.

One evening, Walter asked Aymeric if Monique de Montrepos, Robert's sister, had ever done anything, any sort of work. He met a drowsy, distant stare. Walter had blundered into a private terrain, but the fault was Aymeric's—never posted his limits. Aymeric told scandalous and demeaning stories about his relatives; Walter thought that half of them were invented, just for the purpose of teasing Walter and leading his speculations about the family astray. And yet Aymeric backed off a simple question, something like, "Does Robert's sister work?"

Finally Aymeric yielded and said Monique could infer character from handwriting. Walter's picture of a gypsy in a trailer remained imprinted even after Aymeric assured him that she worked with a team of psychotherapists, in the clean, glassy rooms of a modern office building in Montparnasse. Instead of dropping the matter, Walter wanted to know if she had undergone the proper kind of training; without that, he said, it was the same thing as analyzing handwriting by mail order.

Aymeric thought it over and said that her daughters were well educated and that one of them had travelled to Peru and got on quite well in Peruvian. This time, Walter had sense enough to keep quiet.

By June, Robert's mother had become too difficult for him to manage alone, and so his sister, Monique, who did not live with her husband, turned her apartment over to one of her daughters and moved in to help. Her name was added to the list of tenants hanging from the concierge's doorknob. Walter asked Aymeric if "Montrepos" was a Spanish name. Walter was thinking of the Empress Eugénie, born Montijo, he said.

One would need to consult her husband, Aymeric replied. Aymeric thought that Gaston de Montrepos had been born Dupuy or Dupont or Durand or Dumas. His childhood was spent in one of the weedier Paris suburbs, in a bungalow called Mon Repos. The name was painted, pale green on a rose background, on an enamel plaque just over the doorbell. Most family names had a simple, sentimental origin, if one cared to look them up. (Walter doubted that this applied to Obermauer.) Monique was a perfect specimen of the paratroop aristocracy,

Aymeric went on. He was referring not to a regiment of grandees about to jump in formation but to a recognizable upper-class physical type, stumping along on unbreakable legs. Aymeric represented a more perishable race; the mother with the spun-out surname had left him bones that crumbled, teeth that dissolved in the gum, fine, unbiddable hair. (There was no doubt that Aymeric was haunted by the subject of hair. He combed his own with his fingers all the while he was speaking. The pale tint Walter had observed last March had since been deepened to the yellow of high summer.) Monique's husband had also carried a look of impermanence, in spite of his unassuming background. Monique's father had at first minded about the name. Some simple names he would not have objected to—Rothschild, for instance. He would have let his only daughter be buried as "Monique de Rothschild" any day. Even though. Yes, even though. Gaston had some sort of patronage appointment in the Senate, checking stationery supplies. He had spent most of his working life reading in the Luxembourg when it was fine, and eating coffee éclairs in Pons on rainy afternoons.

After Gaston Dumas or Dupuy had asked for Monique's hand and been turned down, and after Monique had tried to kill herself by taking port wine and four aspirin tablets, Gaston had come back with the news that he was called Montrepos. He showed them something scribbled in his own hand on a leaf torn off a Senate memo pad.

Well, said her father, if Monique wanted that.

Walter soon saw that it was not true about Monique's stumpy legs. For the rest, she was something like Aymeric—blooming, sound. Unlike him, she made free with friendly slaps and punches. Her pat on the back was enough to send one across the room; a knuckle ground into one's arm was a sign of great good spirits. She kissed easily—noisy peasant smacks on both cheeks. She kissed the concierge for bringing good tidings with the morning mail (a check from Gaston, now retired and living in Antibes); kissed Aymeric's cleaning woman for unpaid favors,

such as washing her underclothes. The concierge and the cleaning woman were no more familiar with Monique than with
Robert or Aymeric. If anything, they showed a faint, cautious
reserve. Women who joke and embrace too easily are often quick
to mount a high horse. Of Walter they took the barest notice, in
spite of the size of his tips.

Monique soon overflowed two rooms and a third belonging to
Robert. She shared her mother's bathroom and Robert's kitchen,
striding through Walter's apartment without asking if her perpet-
ual trespassing suited him. In Robert's kitchen she left supper
dishes to soak until morning. Robert could not stand that, and he
washed and dried them before going to bed. Soon after he had
fallen asleep, his mother would come in and ask him what time it
was.

"He was her favorite," Monique told Walter. "Poor Robert.
He's paying for it now. It's a bad idea to be a mother's favorite. It
costs too much later on."

Entering without knocking, Monique let herself fall into one
of Walter's cretonne-covered armchairs. She crossed her legs
and asked if anyone ever bought the stuff one saw in windows of
art galleries. Walter hardly knew how to begin his reply. It would
have encouraged him if Monique had worn clothes that rustled.
Rustle in women's dress, the settling of a skirt as a woman sat
down, smoothing it with both hands, suggested feminine expect-
ancy. Do explain, the taffeta hiss said. Tell about spies, interest
rates, the Americans, Elizabeth Taylor. Is Hitler somewhere, still
alive? But all that was the far past—his boyhood. He had grown
adult in a world where clothes told one nothing. As soon as he
thought of an answer, Monique shouted at him, "What? What
did you say?" When she made a move, it was to knock something
over. In Walter's sitting room she upset a cut-glass decanter,
breaking the stopper; another time it was a mahogany plant stand
and a Chinese pot holding a rare kind of fern. He offered sponge
cakes and watched in distress as she swept the crumbs onto the
floor.

"You've got the best space in the house," she said, looking around.

Soon after that remark, after giving himself time to think about it, Walter started locking all his doors.

M onique and Robert began by discussing Walter's apartment, and moved along to the edge of a quarrel.

"In any case," said Robert, "you should be under your husband's roof. That is the law. You should never have left him."

"Nobody left. It's been like this for years." Monique did not mention that she had come here to help; he knew that. He did not say that he was grateful.

"The law is the law," Robert said.

"Not anymore."

"It was a law when you got married," he said. "The husband is head of the family, he chooses the domicile, the wife is obliged to live under his roof, and he is obliged to receive her there. Under his roof."

"That's finished. If you still bothered to go to weddings, you'd know."

"It was still binding when you married him. He should be offering you a roof."

"He can't," said Monique, flinging out her arm and hitting Robert's record-player, which resisted the shock. "It's about to cave in from the weight of the mortgage."

"Well," said Robert, forgetting Gaston for a moment, "he has a lease and he pays his rent regularly. And I am still paying for mending *my* roof." After a pause he said, "Aymeric says Gaston has a rich woman in Antibes."

"I was said to have been a rich young one."

"There is space for you here, always," said Robert instantly. There would be even more, later on. When the time came, they would knock all the flats into one and divide up the new space obtained.

"Look up 'harp' in your dream book," she said. "I dreamed I
was giving a concert."

R obert usually got the dream book out on Sundays. The others
saved up their weeknight dreams. Aymeric continued to
dream he had been slighted. It was a dream of contradiction, and
meant that in real life he was deeply appreciated. Robert's
mother dreamed she was polishing furniture, which prophesied
good luck with the opposite sex. Monique played tennis in a
downpour: her affections would be returned. Robert went to
answer the doorbell—the sign of a happy surprise. They began
each new week reassured and smiling—all but Walter. He had
been dreaming about moles and dormice again.

As the summer weather settled in, and with Monique there to
care for their mother, Robert began spending weekends out of
town. He took the Dijon train at the Gare de Lyon and got off at
Tonnerre. Monique found cancelled railway tickets in waste-
paper baskets. Walter had a sudden illumination: Robert must be
attending weekend retreats in a monastery. That thin, quiet face
belonged to a world of silence. Then, one day, Robert mentioned
that there was a ballooning club in Tonnerre. Balloons were
quieter than helicopters. Swaying in silence, between the clouds
and the Burgundy Canal, he had been able to reach a decision.
He did not say what about.

He accepted books from Walter to read in the train. They
piled up at his bedside as he kept forgetting to give them back.
Some he owned up to having lost. Walter could see them
overhead, St. Augustine and St. Thomas Aquinas, drifting and
swaying. He had no wish to ascend in a balloon. He had seen
enough balloons in engravings. Virtually anything portrayed as
art turned his stomach. There was hardly anything he could look
at without feeling sick. In any case, Robert did not invite him.

Sometimes they watched television together. Aymeric had an
old black-and-white set with only two channels. Monique had a

Japanese portable, but the screen was too small for her mother to enjoy. They all liked Walter's set, which had a large screen and more buttons than there would ever be channels in France. One Saturday when Robert was not ballooning, he suddenly said he was getting married. It was just in the middle of "Dallas." They were about a year behind Switzerland, and Monique had been asking Walter, whose occasional trips to Bern kept him up-to-date, to tell them how it would all turn out. Aymeric switched off the sound, upon which Robert's mother went straight to sleep.

Robert said only that his first marriage had been so happy that he could hardly wait to start over. The others sat staring at him. Walter had a crazy idea, which he kept to himself: Would Robert get married overhead in a balloon? "I am happy," Robert said, once or twice. Walter fixed his eyes on the bright, silent screen.

Monique prepared their mother's meals and carried them from Robert's kitchen on a tray. She had to make a wide detour around Walter's locked apartment. Everything was stone cold by the time the old lady had been coaxed to sit down. Their mother had her own kitchen, but she filled the oven with whatever came to hand when she was tidying—towels, a shoebox full of old Bic pens. Once, Monique found a bolster folded in two, looking like a bloated loaf. She disconnected the stove, so that her mother could not turn on the gas and start a fire.

Robert showed them a picture of his bride-to-be. She and Robert stood smiling, with arms linked, both wearing track suits. "Does she run as well as float?" said Aymeric. He turned the snapshot over and read a date and the initial "B."

"Brigitte," said Robert.

"Brigitte what?"

"I don't want anyone driving to Tonnerre for long talks," said Robert. He did say that she taught French grammar to semi-delinquents in a technical high school. She was trying to obtain a transfer to a Paris suburb. There could be no question of the Capital itself: one had to know someone, and there was a waiting list ten years long.

Monique's arrival was followed closely by a new shock from the administrative authorities of Paris: a telephone number old people could call in the summertime, free of charge, in case their families were away and they felt lonely. Robert's mother dialled the number on Aymeric's phone. The woman at the other end—young, from the sound of her—seemed surprised to hear that Robert's mother lived with a son, a daughter, and a nephew, all attentive; had the use of a large television set with plenty of buttons and dials; and still suffered from feelings of neglect and despair. She was afraid of dying alone in the dark. All night long, she tried to stay on her feet.

The young voice reminded her about old people who had absolutely no one, who lived at the top of six steep flights of stairs, who did not dare go down to buy a packet of macaroni for fear of the long climb back. Robert's mother replied that the lives of such people were at the next-to-final stage of hopelessness and terror. Her own meals were brought to her on a tray. She was not claiming more for her sentiments than blind panic.

Aymeric took the telephone out of her hand, said a few words into it, and hung up. His aunt gave him her sweet, steady smile before remarking, "Your poor mother, Aymeric, was nothing much to look at."

W alter, trying to find a place to go for his summer holiday where there would be no reminders of art, fell back on Switzerland and his mother and father. He scrubbed and vacu-umed his rooms and put plastic dust sheets over the furniture. Just before calling for a taxi to take him to the airport, he asked Robert if he could have a word with him. He was more than usually nervous, and kept flexing his hands. Terrible things had been said at the gallery that day; Walter had threatened his employer with the police. Robert could not understand the story—something incoherent to do with the office safe. He removed a bundle of clothes fresh from the launderette (he did his own ironing) and invited Walter to sit down. Walter wanted to know if the imminent change in Robert's life and Monique's constant hints about the best space in the house meant that Walter's apartment was coveted. "Coveted" was a heavy word, but Robert finally answered, "You've got your lease."

"According to the law," said Walter, more and more fussed, "you can throw me out if you can prove you need the space." Robert sat quietly, and seemed to be waiting for something else. "I've got to be sure I have a home to come back to—a home I can keep for a long time. This time I really intend to give notice. I don't care about the pension. He's making me an accomplice in crime. I'll stay just until he can train a replacement for me. If he sees I am worried about something else as well, it will give him the upper hand. And then, I'm like you and Aymeric. I feel as if my own family had been living here forever." Robert at this looked at him with a terrible politeness. Walter rushed on, mentioning a matter that other tenants, he thought, would have brought up first. Since moving in, he had painted the kitchen, paved the bathroom with imported tiles, and hung custom-made curtains on rods designed to fit the windows. All this, he said, constituted an embellishment of space.

"Your vacation will do you good," said Robert.

Walter gave Robert his house keys and said he hoped Monique would feel free to use his apartment as a passageway while he was gone. Handing them over, he was reminded of another gesture—his hand, outstretched, opening to reveal the snuffbox.

Their mother had begun polishing furniture, as in some of her dreams. A table in Walter's sitting room was like a pond. Everything else was dusty. The plastic sheets lay like crumpled parachutes in a corner. On Aymeric's birthday, late in August, he and Robert and Monique sat at the polished table eating pastries out of a box. Robert picked out a few of the kind his mother liked and put them aside for her on a plate. They could hear her, in Walter's bedroom, telling City Hall that they had disconnected her stove.

Perhaps because there was an empty chair, Robert suddenly said that Brigitte was immensely sociable and liked to entertain. She played first-class bridge. She had somehow managed to obtain a transfer to Paris after all. They would be getting married in October.

"How did she do it?" Aymeric asked.

"She knows someone."

They fell silent, admiring the empty chair.

"Who wants the last strawberry tart?" said Monique. When no one answered, she cut it in three.

"We will have to rearrange the space," said Robert. He traced lines with his finger on the polished table and, with the palm of his hand, wiped something out.

Aymeric said, "Try to find out what she did with that snuffbox. I wanted to give it to you as a wedding present."

"I'll look again in the oven," Monique said.

"Ask her carefully," said Aymeric. "Don't frighten her. Sometimes she remembers."

Robert went on tracing invisible lines.

W̶alter came back in September to find his kitchen under occupation, full of rusted sieves and food mills and old graters. On the stove was a saucepan of strained soup for the old woman's supper; a bowl of pureed apricots stood uncovered in the sink. He removed everything to the old woman's kitchen.

I was brought up so soundly, he said to himself. He had respected his parents; now he admired them. At home, nothing had made him feel worried or tense, and he hadn't minded his father's habit of reading the newspaper aloud while Walter tried to watch television. When his father answered the telephone, his mother called, "What do they want?" from the kitchen. His father always repeated everything the caller said, so that his mother would not miss a word of the conversation. There were no secrets, no mysteries. What Walter saw of his parents was probably all there was.

After cleaning his rooms and unpacking his suitcase, Walter called on Robert. He had meant to ask how they had spent their holidays, if in spite of the old lady they had managed to get away, but instead he found himself telling about a remarkable dream he'd had in Switzerland: A large badger had burst into the gallery and taken Walter's employer hostage. Trout Face had said, "You're not getting away with this. I'm not having anybody running around here with automatic weapons." It was not a nightmare, said Walter. He had seen himself, aloof and nonchalant, enjoying the incident.

Robert said he would look it up. That night he made a neat stack of the books Walter had lent him—all that he could still find—and left it outside his locked front door. He wrote on the back of a page torn off a calendar, "Dream of badger taking man hostage means a change of residence, for which the dreamer should be prepared. R." He rewrote this several times, changing a word here and there. In the morning, after starting the record and opening all the windows, he sat down and read his message again. He kept running his finger over the note, as he had traced new boundaries on Walter's table, and seemed to be wondering if there was any point in trying to say the same thing some other way.

LUC AND HIS FATHER

To the astonishment of no one except his father and mother, Luc Clairevoie failed the examination that should have propelled him straight into one of the finest schools of engineering in Paris; failed it so disastrously, in fact, that an examiner, who knew someone in the same ministry as Luc's father, confided it was the sort of labor in vain that should be written up. Luc's was a prime case of universal education gone crazy. He was a victim of the current belief that any student, by dint of application, could answer what he was asked.

Luc's father blamed the late President de Gaulle. If de Gaulle had not opened the schools and universities to hordes of qualified but otherwise uninteresting young people, teachers would have had more time to spare for Luc. De Gaulle had been dead for years, but Roger Clairevoie still suspected him of cosmic mischief and double-dealing. (Like his wife, Roger had never got over the loss of Algeria. When the price of fresh fruit went high, as it did every winter, the Clairevoies told each other it was because of the loss of all those Algerian orchards.)

Where Luc was concerned, they took a practical course,

lowered their sights to a lesser but still elegant engineering school, and sent Luc to a crammer for a year to get ready for a new trial. His mother took Luc to the dentist, had his glasses changed, and bought him a Honda 125 to make up for his recent loss of self-esteem. Roger's contribution took the form of long talks. Cornering Luc in the kitchen after breakfast, or in his own study, now used as a family television room, Roger told Luc how he had been graduated with honors from the noblest engineering institute in France; how he could address other alumni using the second person singular, even by Christian name, regardless of whether they spoke across a ministerial desk or a lunch table. Many of Roger's fellow-graduates had chosen civil-service careers. They bumped into one another in marble halls, under oil portraits of public servants who wore the steadfast look of advisers to gods; and these distinguished graduates, Roger among them, had a charming, particular way of seeming like brothers—or so it appeared to those who could only envy them, who had to keep to "Have I the honor of" and "If Mr. Assistant Under-Secretary would be good enough to" and "Should it suit the convenience." To this fraternity Luc could no longer aspire, but there was still some hope for future rank and dignity: he could become an engineer in the building trades. Luc did not reply; he did not even ask, "Do you mean houses, or garages, or what?" Roger supposed he was turning things over in his mind.

The crammer he went to was a brisk, costly examination factory in Rennes, run by Jesuits, with the reputation for being able to jostle any student, even the dreamiest, into a respectable institute for higher learning. The last six words were from the school's brochure. They ran through Roger Clairevoie's head like an election promise.

Starting in September, Luc spent Monday to Friday in Rennes. Weekends, he came home by train, laden with books, and shut himself up to study. Sometimes Roger would hear him trying chords on his guitar: pale sound without rhythm or sequence. When Luc had studied enough, he buckled on his white helmet and roared around Paris on the Honda. (The promise of a BMW R/80 was in the air, as reward or consolation, depending on next year's results.) On the helmet Luc had lettered "IN CASE OF ACCIDENT DO NOT REMOVE." "You see, he does think of things," his mother said. "Luc thinks of good, useful things."

Like many Parisian students, Luc was without close friends, and in Rennes he knew nobody. His parents were somewhat relieved when, in the autumn, he became caught like a strand of seaweed on the edge of a political discussion group. The group met every Sunday afternoon in some member's house. Once, the group assembled at the Clairevoies'; Simone Clairevoie, pleased to see that Luc was showing interest in adult problems, served fruit juice, pâté sandwiches, and two kinds of ice cream. Luc's friends did not paint slogans on the sidewalk, or throw petrol bombs at police stations, or carry weapons (at least, Roger hoped not), or wear ragtag uniforms bought at the flea market. A few old men talked, and the younger men, those Luc's age, sat on a windowsill or on the floor, and seemed to listen. Among the speakers the day they came to the Clairevoies' was a retired journalist, once thought ironic and alarming, and the former secretary of a minor visionary, now in decrepit exile in Spain. Extremist movements were banned, but, as Roger pointed out to his wife, one could not really call this a movement. There was no law against meeting on a winter afternoon to consider the false starts of history. Luc never said much, but his parents supposed he must be taking to heart the message of the failed old men; and it was curious to see how Luc could grasp a slippery, allusive message so easily when he could not keep in mind his own private destiny as an engineer. Luc could vote, get married without permission, have his own bank account, run up bills. He could leave home, though a course so eccentric had probably not yet occurred to him. He was of age; adult; a grown man.

The Clairevoies had spent their married life in an apartment on the second floor of a house of venturesome design, built just after the First World War, in a quiet street near the Bois de

Boulogne. The designer of the house, whose name they could never recall, had been German or Austrian. Roger, when questioned by colleagues surprised to find him in surroundings so bizarre, would say, "The architect was Swiss," which made him sound safer. Students of architecture rang the bell to ask if they might visit the rooms and take photographs. Often they seemed taken aback by the sight of the furniture, a wedding gift from Roger's side of the family, decorated with swans and sphinxes; the armchairs were as hard and uncompromising as the Judgment Seat. To Roger, the furniture served as counterpoise to the house, which belonged to the alien Paris of the nineteen-twenties, described by Roger's father as full of artists and immigrants of a shiftless kind—the flotsam of Europe.

The apartment, a wedding present from Simone's parents, was her personal choice. Roger's people, needing the choice explained away, went on saying for years that Simone had up-to-date ideas; but Roger was not sure this was true. After all, the house was some forty years old by the time the Clairevoies moved in. The street, at least, barely changed from year to year, unless one counted the increasing number of prostitutes that drifted in from the Bois. Directly across from the house, a café, the only place of business in sight, served as headquarters for the prostitutes' rest periods, conversations, and quarrels. Sometimes Roger went there when he ran out of cigarettes. He knew some of the older women by sight, and he addressed them courteously; and they, of course, were polite to him. Once, pausing under the awning to light a cigarette, he glanced up and saw Luc standing at a window, the curtain held aside with an elbow. He seemed to be staring at nothing in particular, merely waiting for something that might fix his attention. Roger had a middle-aged, paternal reflex: Is that what he calls studying? If Luc noticed his father, he gave no sign.

Simone Clairevoie called it the year of shocks. There had been Luc's failure, then Roger had suffered a second heart attack,

infinitely more frightening than the first. He was home all day on
convalescent leave from his ministry, restless and bored, smoking
on the sly, grudgingly walking the family dog by way of moderate
exercise. Finally, even though all three Clairevoies had voted
against it, a Socialist government came to power. Simone foresaw nothing but further decline. If Luc failed again, it would
mean a humble career, preceded by a tour of Army duty—plain
military service, backpack and drill, with the sons of peasants and
Algerian delinquents. Roger would never be able to get him out
of it: he knew absolutely no one in the new system of favors.
Those friends whose careers had not been lopped sat hard on
their jobs, almost afraid to pick up the telephone. Every call was
bad news. The worst news would be the voice of an old acquaintance, harking back to a foundered regime and expecting a good
turn. Although the Clairevoies seldom went to church now—the
new Mass was the enemy—Simone prayed hard on Christmas
Eve, singling out in particular St. Odile, who had been useful in
the past, around a time when Roger had seemed to regret his
engagement to Simone and may have wanted to break it off.

Soon after the New Year, however, there came a message
from the guidance counsellor of the Jesuit school, summoning
the Clairevoies for "a frank and open discussion."

"About being immortal?" said Roger to Simone, recalling an
alarming talk with another Jesuit teacher long ago.

"About your son," she replied.

A card on his door identified the counsellor as "F.-X.
Rousseau, Orientation." Orientation wore a track suit and did
not look to Roger like a Jesuit, or even much like a priest.
Leaning forward (the Clairevoies instinctively drew back), he
offered American cigarettes before lighting his own. It was not
Luc's chances of passing that seemed to worry him but Luc's
fragmented image of women. On the Rorschach test, for
instance, he had seen a ballet skirt and a pair of legs, and a female
head in a fishing net.

"You brought me here to tell me what?" said Roger. "My son
has poor eyesight?"

Simone placed her hand on Father Rousseau's desk as she might have touched his sleeve. She was saying, Be careful. My husband is irritable, old-fashioned, ill. "I think that Father Rousseau is trying to tell us that Luc has no complete view of women because Luc has no complete view of himself as a man. Is that it?"

Father Rousseau added, "And he cannot see his future because he can't see himself."

It was Roger's turn to remonstrate with Luc. Simone suggested masculine, virile surroundings for their talk, and so he took Luc to the café across the street. There, over beer for Luc and mineral water for Roger, he told Luc about satisfaction. It was the duty of children to satisfy their parents. Roger, by doing extremely well at his studies, had given Luc's grandparents this mysterious pleasure. They had been able to tell their friends, "Roger has given us great satisfaction." He took Luc on a fresh tour of things to come, showing him the slow-grinding machinery of state competitive examinations against which fathers measured their sons. He said, Your future. If you fail. A poor degree is worse than none. Thousands of embittered young men, all voting Socialist. If you fail, you will sink into the swamp from which there is no rising. Do you want to sell brooms? Sweep the streets? Sell tickets in the Métro? Do you want to spend your life in a bank?

"Not that there is anything wrong with working in a bank," he corrected. Encrusted in his wife's family was a small rural bank with a staff of seventeen. Simone did not often see her provincial cousins, but the bank was always mentioned with respect. To say "a small bank" was no worse than saying "a small crown jewel." Simone, in a sense, personified a reliable and almost magical trade; she had brought to Roger the goods and the dream. What had Roger brought? Hideous Empire furniture and a dubious nineteenth-century title Simone scarcely dared use because of the Communists.

Only the word "Socialist" seemed to stir Luc. "We need a good little civil war," he declared, as someone who has never been near the ocean might announce, "We need a good little tidal wave"—so Roger thought.

He said, "There are no good little civil wars." But he knew what was said of him: that his heart attacks had altered his personality, made him afraid. On a November day, Roger and his father had followed the coffin of Charles Maurras, the nationalist leader, jailed after the war for collaboration. "My son," said Roger's father, introducing Roger to thin-faced men, some wearing the Action Française emblem. Roger's father had stood for office on a Royalist platform, and had come out of the election the last of five candidates, one an impertinent youngster with an alien name, full of "z"'s and "k"'s. He was not bitter; he was scornful and dry, and he wanted Roger to be dry and proud. Roger had only lately started to think, My father always said, and, My father believed. As he spoke, now, to Luc about satisfaction and failure, he remembered how he had shuffled behind the hearse of a dead old man, perhaps mistaken, certainly dispossessed. They got up to leave, and Roger bowed to an elderly woman he recognized. His son had already turned away.

In order to give Luc a fully virile image, Simone redecorated his room. The desk lamp was a galleon in full sail with a bright red shade—the color of decision and activity. She took down the photograph of Roger's graduating class and hung a framed poster of Che Guevara. Stepping back to see the effect, she realized Guevara would never do. The face was feminine, soft. She wondered if the whole legend was not a hoax and if Guevara had been a woman in disguise. Guevara had no political significance, of course; he had become manly, decorative kitsch. (The salesman had assured her of this; otherwise, she would never have run the risk of offending Roger.) As she removed the poster she noticed for the first time a hole drilled in the wall. She put her eye to it and had a partial view of the maid's bathroom, used in the past by a succession of *au pair* visitors, in Paris to improve their French and to keep an eye on a younger Luc.

She called Roger and made him look: "Who says Luc has no view of women?"

Roger glanced round at the new curtains and bedspread, with their pattern of Formula 1 racing cars. Near the bed someone—Luc, probably—had tacked a photo of Hitler. Roger, without saying anything, took it down. He did not want Luc quite that manly.

"You can't actually see the shower," said Simone, trying the perspective again. "But I suppose that when she stands drying on the mat...We'd better tell him."

"Tell Luc?"

"Rousseau. Orientation."

Not "Father Rousseau," he noticed. It was not true that women were devoted guardians of tradition. They rode every new wave like so much plankton. My father was right, he decided. He always said it was a mistake to give them the vote. He said they had no ideas—just notions. My father was proud to stand up for the past. He was proud to be called a Maurrassien, even when Charles Maurras was in defeat, in disgrace. But who has ever heard of a Maurrassienne? The very idea made Roger smile. Simone, catching the smile, took it to mean a sudden feeling of tolerance, and so she chose the moment to remind him they would have an *au pair* guest at Easter—oh, not to keep an eye on Luc; Luc was too old. (She sounded sorry.) But Luc had been three times to England, to a family named Brunt, and now, in all fairness, it was the Clairevoies' obligation to have Cassandra.

"Another learner?" Roger was remembering the tall, glum girls from northern capitals and their strides in colloquial French: That is my friend. He did not sleep in my bed—he spent the night on the doormat. I am homesick. I am ill. A bee has stung me. I am allergic and may die.

"You won't have to worry about Cassandra," Simone said. "She is a mature young woman of fifteen, a whole head taller than Luc."

Simone clipped a leash to the dog's collar and grasped Roger firmly by the arm. She was taking two of her charges for a walk, along streets she used to follow when Luc was still in his pram.

On Boulevard Lannes a taxi stopped and two men wearing white furs, high-heeled white boots, and Marilyn Monroe wigs got out and made for the Bois. Roger knew that transvestites worked the fringe of the Bois now, congregating mostly toward the Porte Maillot, where there were hotels. He had heard the women in the café across the street complaining that the police were not vigilant enough, much the way an established artisan might grumble about black-market labor. Roger had imagined them vaguely as night creatures, glittering and sequined, caught like dragonflies in the headlights of roving automobiles. This pair was altogether real, and the man who had just paid the taxi-driver shut his gold-mesh handbag with the firm snap of a housewife settling the butcher's bill. The dog at once began to strain and bark.

"Brazilians," said Simone, who watched educational television in the afternoon. "They send all their money home."

"But in broad daylight," said Roger.

"They don't earn as much as you think."

"There could be little children playing in the Bois."

"We can't help our children by living in the past," said Simone. Roger wondered if she was having secret talks with Father Rousseau. "Stop that," she told the barking dog.

"He's not deliberately trying to hurt their feelings," Roger said. Because he disliked animals—in particular, dogs—he tended to make excuses for the one they owned. Actually, the dog was an accident in their lives, purchased only after the staff psychologist in Luc's old school had said the boy's grades were poor because he had no siblings to love and hate, no rivals for his parents' attention, no responsibility to any living creature.

"A dog will teach my son to add and subtract?" said Roger. Simone had wondered if a dog would make Luc affectionate and polite, more grateful for his parents' devotion, aware of the many sacrifices they had made on his behalf.

Yes, yes, they had been assured. A dog could do all that.

Luc was twelve years old, the puppy ten weeks. Encouraged to find a name for him, Luc came up with "Mongrel." Simone chose "Sylvestre." Sylvestre spent his first night in Luc's room—part of the night, that is. When he began to whine, Luc put him out. After that, Sylvestre was fed, trained, and walked by Luc's parents, while Luc continued to find school a mystery and to show indifference and ingratitude. Want of thanks is a parent's lot, but blindness to simple arithmetic was like an early warning of catastrophe. Luc's parents had already told him he was to train as an engineer.

"Do you know how stiff the competition is?" his mother asked.

"Yes."

"Do you want to be turned down by the best schools?"

"I don't know."

"Do you want to be sent to a third-rate school, miles from home? Have you thought about that?"

Roger leaned on Simone, though he did not need to, and became querulous: "Sylvestre and I are two old men."

This was not what Simone liked to talk about. She said, "Your family never took you into consideration. You slept in your father's study. You took second best."

"It didn't feel that way."

"Look at our miserable country house. Look at your Cousin Henri's estate."

"His godmother gave it to him," said Roger, as though she needed reminding.

"He should have given you compensation."

"People don't do that," said Roger. "All I needed was a richer godmother."

"The apartment is mine," said Simone, as they walked arm in arm. "The furniture is yours. The house in the country is yours, but most of the furniture belongs to me. You paid for the pool and the tennis court." It was not unpleasant conversation.

Roger stopped in front of a pastry shop and showed Simone a chocolate cake. "Why can't we have that?"

"Because it would kill you. The specialist said so."

"We could have oysters," Roger said. "I'm allowed oysters."

"Luc will be home," said Simone. "He doesn't like them."

Father Rousseau sent for the Clairevoies again. This time he wore a tweed jacket over a white sweater, with a small crucifix on one lapel and a Solidarność badge on the other. After lighting his cigarette he sat drumming his fingers, as if wondering how to put his grim news into focus. At last he said, "No one can concentrate on an exam and on a woman. Not at the same time."

"Women?" cried Simone. "What women?"

"Woman," Roger corrected, unheard.

There was a woman in Luc's life. It seemed unbelievable, but it was so.

"French?" said Roger instantly.

Father Rousseau was unable to swear to it. Her name was Katia, her surname Martin, but if Martin was the most common family name in France it might be because so many foreigners adopted it.

"I can find out," Simone interrupted. "What's her age?"

Katia was eighteen. Her parents were divorced.

"That's bad," said Simone. "Who's her father?"

She lived in Biarritz with her mother, but came often to Paris to stay with her father and brother. Her brother belonged to a political debating society.

"I've seen him," said Simone. "I know the one. She's a terrorist. Am I right?"

Father Rousseau doubted it. "She is a spoiled, rich, undereducated young woman, used to having her own way. She is also very much in love."

"With Luc?" said Roger.

"Luc is a Capricorn," said Simone. "The most levelheaded of all the signs."

So was Katia, Father Rousseau said. She and Luc wrote "Capricorn loves Capricorn" in the dust on parked cars.

"Does Luc want to marry her?" said Simone, getting over the worst.

"He wants something." But Father Rousseau hoped it would not be Katia. She seemed to have left school early, after a number of misadventures. She was hardly the person to inspire Luc, who needed a model he could copy. When Katia was around, Luc did not even pretend to study. When she was in Biarritz, he waited for letters. The two collected lump sugar from cafés but seemed to have no other cultural interest.

"She's from a rich family?" Simone said. "And she has just the one brother?"

"Luc has got to pass his entrance examination," said Roger. "After he gets his degree he can marry anyone he likes."

"'Rich' is a relative term," said Simone, implying that Father Rousseau was too unworldly to define such a thing.

Roger said, "How do you know about the sugar and 'Capricorn loves Capricorn' and how Luc and Katia got to know each other?"

"Why, from Katia's letters, of course," said Father Rousseau, sounding surprised.

"Did you keep copies?" said Simone.

"Do you know that Luc is of age, and that he could take you to court for reading his mail?" said Roger.

Father Rousseau turned to Simone, the rational parent. "Not a word of reproach," he warned her. "Just keep an eye on the situation. We feel that Luc should spend the next few weeks at home, close to his parents." He would come back to Rennes just before the examination, for last-minute heavy cramming. Roger understood this to be a smooth Jesuitical manner of getting rid of Luc.

Luc came home, and no one reproached him. He promised to work hard and proposed going alone to the country house, which was near Auxerre. Simone objected that the place had been unheated all winter. Luc replied that he would live in one room and take his meals in the village. Roger guessed that Luc intended to spend a good amount of time with Cousin Henri,

who lived nearby, and whom Luc—no one knew why—professed
to admire. Cousin Henri and Roger enjoyed property litigation
of long standing, but as there was a dim, far chance of Henri's
leaving something to Luc, Roger said nothing. And as Simone
pointed out, meaning by this nothing unkind or offensive, any
male model for Luc was better than none.

In the meantime, letters from Katia, forwarded from Rennes,
arrived at the Paris apartment. Roger watched in pure amazement the way Simone managed to open them, rolling a kitchen
match under the flap. Having read the letter, she resealed it
without trace. The better the quality of the paper, the easier the
match trick, she explained. She held a page up to the light,
approving the watermark.

"We'll need a huge apartment, because we will have so many
children," Katia wrote. "And we'll need space for the sugar
collection."

The only huge apartment Simone could think of was her own.
"They wish we were dead," she told Roger. "My son wishes I
were out of the way." She read aloud, " 'What would you be
without me? One more little Frenchman, eternally studying for
exams.' "

"What does she mean by 'little Frenchman'?" said Roger. He
decided that Katia must be foreign—a descendant of White
Russians, perhaps. There had been a colony in Biarritz in his
father's day, the men gambling away their wives' tiaras before
settling down as headwaiters and croupiers. Luc was entangled in
a foreign love affair; he was already alien, estranged. Roger had
seen him standing at the window, like an idle landowner in a
Russian novel. What did Roger know about Russians? There
were the modern ones, dressed in gray, with bulldog faces; there
were the slothful, mournful people in books, the impulsive and
slender women, the indecisive men. But it had been years since
Roger had opened a novel; what he saw were overlapping
images, like stills from old films.

" 'Where are you, where are you?' " read Simone. " 'There is
a light in your parents' room, but your windows are dark. I'm

standing under the awning across the street. My shoes are soaked. I am too miserable to care.'

"She can't be moping in the rain and writing all at the same time," said Simone. "And the postmark is Biarritz. She comes to Paris to stir up trouble. How does she know which room is ours? Luc is probably sick of her. He must have been at a meeting."

Yes, he had probably been at a meeting, sitting on the floor of a pale room, with a soft-voiced old man telling him about an older, truer Europe. Luc was learning a Europe caught in amber, unchanging, with trees for gods. There was no law against paganism and politics, or soft-voiced old men.

At least there are no guns, Roger told himself. And where had Simone learned the way to open other people's letters? He marvelled at Katia's doing for his son what no woman had ever done for him; she had stood in the rain, crying probably, watching for a light.

Ten days before Easter, Cassandra Brunt arrived. Her father was a civil servant, like Roger. He was also an author: two books had been published, one about Napoleon's retreat from Moscow, the other about the failure of the Maginot Line and the disgraceful conduct of the French officer class. Both had been sent to the Clairevoies, with courteous inscriptions. When Simone had gone over to England alone, to see if the Brunts would do for Luc, Mrs. Brunt confided that her husband was more interested in the philosophy of combat than in success and defeat. He was a dreamer, and that was why he had never got ahead. Simone replied that Roger, too, had been hampered by guiding principles. As a youth, he had read for his own pleasure. His life was a dream. Mrs. Brunt suggested a major difference: Mr. Brunt was no full-time dreamer. He had written five books, two of which had been printed, one in 1952 and one in 1966. The two women had then considered each other's child, decided it was sexless and safe and that Luc and Cassandra could spend time under the same roof. After that, Luc crossed the Channel for three visits, while Simone managed not to have Cassandra even once. Her excuse was the extreme youth of Cassandra and the dangers of Paris. Now that Cassandra was fifteen Mrs. Brunt, suddenly exercising her sense of things owed, had written to say that Cassandra was ready for perils and the French.

Roger and Simone met Cassandra at the Gare du Nord. The moment he saw her, Roger understood she had been forced by her parents to make the trip, and that they were ruining her Easter holiday. He marvelled that a fifteen-year-old of her size and apparent strength could be bullied into anything.

"I'll be seeing Luc, what fun," said Cassandra, jackknifed into the car, her knees all but touching her chin. "It will be nice to see Luc," she said sadly. Her fair hair almost covered her face.

"Luc is at our country residence, studying with all the strength of his soul," said Simone. "He is in the Yonne," she added. Cassandra looked puzzled. Roger supposed that to a foreigner it must sound as though Luc had fallen into a river.

There had been no coaxing Luc, no pleading; no threat was strong enough to frighten him. They could keep the BMW; they could stop his allowance; they could put him in jail. He would not come to Paris to welcome Cassandra. He was through with England, through with the Brunts—through, for that matter, with his mother and father. Katia had taken their place.

"We'll have her in Paris for a week, alone," Simone had wailed. Luc's argument was unassailable; alone, he could study. Once they were all there, he would have to be kind to Cassandra, making conversation and showing her the village church. Simone put the blame on Mrs. Brunt, who had insisted in a wholly obtuse way on having her rights.

"How are your delicious parents?" she asked, turning as well as the seat belt allowed, seeming to let the car drive itself in Paris traffic.

"Daddy's at home now. He's retired from the minstrel."

"The ministry," said Simone deeply. Cassandra's was the only English she had ever completely understood. "My husband has

also retired from public service. It was too much for his heart. He
is much younger than Mr. Brunt, I believe."

"Daddy was a late starter," said Cassandra. "But he'll last a
long time. At least, I hope so."

Like the dog bought to improve Luc's arithmetic; like the
tropical fish Simone had tended for Luc, and eventually
mourned; like the tennis court in which Luc had at once lost
interest and on which Roger had had his first heart attack, so
Cassandra fell to Luc's parents. With Simone, she watched
television; with Roger, she walked uphill and down, to parks and
museums.

"What was your minstrel?" she asked Roger, as they marched
toward the Bois.

"Years ago, when there was a grave shortage of telephones,
thanks to President de Gaulle—" Roger began. "Do you recall
that unhappy time?"

"I'm afraid I'm dreffly ignorant."

"I was good at getting friends off the waiting list. That was
what I did best."

He clutched her arm, dragging her out of the way of buses and
taxis that rushed from the left while Cassandra looked hopelessly
right.

"You like the nature?" he said, letting Sylvestre run free in the
Bois. "The trees?"

"My mother does. Though this is hardly nature, is it?"

Sylvestre loped, snuffling, into a club of dusty shrubbery. He
gave a yelp and came waddling out. All Roger saw of the person
who had kicked him was a flash of white boot.

"You have them in England?" said Roger.

"Have what?"

"That. Male, female. Prostitutes."

"Yes, of course. But they aren't vile to animals."

"You like the modern art?" Roger asked, breathless, as they
plodded up the stalled escalators of the Beaubourg museum.

"I'm horribly old-fashioned, I'm afraid."

Halfway, he paused to let his heart rest. His heart was an old pump, clogged and filthy. Cassandra's heart was of bright new metal; it beat more quietly and regularly than any clock.

Above the city stretched a haze of pollution, unstirring, all of an even color. The sun suffused the haze with amber dye, which by some grim alchemy was turned into dun. Roger saw through the haze to a forgotten city, unchanging, and it was enough to wrench the heart. A hand, reaching inside the rib cage, seemed to grasp the glutted machine. He knew that some part of the machine was intact, faithful to him; when his heart disowned him entirely he might as well die.

Cassandra, murmuring that looking down made her feel giddy, turned her back. Roger watched a couple, below, walking hand in hand. He was too far away to see their faces. They were eating out of a shared paper bag. The young man looked around, perhaps for a bin. Finding none, he handed the bag to the girl, who flung it down. The two were dressed nearly alike, in blue jackets and jeans. Simone had assured Roger that Katia was French, but he still saw her Russian. He saw Katia in winter furs, with a fur hat, and long fair hair over a snowy collar. She removed a glove and gave the hand, warm, to Luc to hold.

"I'm afraid I must be getting lazy," Cassandra remarked. "I found that quite a climb."

The couple in blue had turned a corner. Of Luc and Katia there remained footsteps on lightly fallen snow.

"This place reminds me of a giant food processor," said Cassandra. "What does it make you think of?"

"Young lovers," Roger said.

Cassandra had a good point in Simone's eyes: she kept a diary, which Simone used to improve her English.

"The Baron has sex on the brain," Simone read. "Even a museum reminds him of sex. In the Bois de Boulogne he tried to twist the conversation around to sex and bestiality. You have to be careful every minute. Each time we have to cross the road he tries to squeeze my arm."

W hen Cassandra had been shown enough of Paris, Simone packed the car with food that Luc liked to eat and drove south and east with the dog, Roger, and Cassandra. They stopped often during the journey so that Cassandra, who sat in the back of the car, could get out and be sick. They found Luc living like an elderly squatter in a ground-floor room full of toast crusts. It was three in the afternoon, and he was still wearing pajamas. Inevitably, Cassandra asked if he was ill.

"Katia's been here," said Simone, going round the house and opening shutters. "I can tell. It's in the air."

Luc was occupying the room meant for Cassandra. He showed no willingness to give it up. He took slight notice of his parents, and none whatever of their guest. It seemed to Roger that he had grown taller, but this was surely an illusion, a psychological image in Roger's mind. His affair, if Roger could call it that, had certainly made him bolder. He mentioned Katia by name, saying that one advantage of living alone was that he could read his mail before anyone else got to it. Roger foresaw a holiday of bursting quarrels. He supposed Cassandra would go home and tell her father, the historian, that the French were always like that.

On the day they arrived, Simone intercepted and read a letter. Katia, apparently in answer to some questioning from Luc, explained that she had almost, but not entirely, submitted to the advances of a cousin. (Luc, to forestall his mother, met the postman at the gate. Simone, to short-circuit Luc, had already picked up the letters that interested her at the village post office.) Katia's near-seduction had taken place in a field of barley, while her cousin was on leave from military service. A lyrical account of clouds, birds, and crickets took up most of a page.

Roger would not touch the letter, but he listened as Simone read aloud. It seemed to him that some coarse appreciation of the cousin was concealed behind all those crickets and birds. Katia's blithe candor was insolent, a slur on his son. At the same time, he took heart: If a cousin was liable for Army duty, some part of the family must be French. On the other hand, who would rape his cousin in a barley field, if not a Russian?

"You swore Katia was French," he said, greatly troubled.

He knew nothing of Katia, but he did know something about fields. Roger decided he did not believe a word of the story. Katia was trying to turn Luc into a harmless and impotent bachelor friend. The two belonged in a novel of the early nineteen-fifties. (Simone, as Roger said this, began to frown.) "Luc is the good, kind man she can tell stories to," he said. "Her stories will be more and more about other men." As Simone drew breath, he said quickly, "Not that I see Luc in a novel."

"No, but I can see you in the diary of a hysterical English girl," said Simone, and she told him about Cassandra.

Roger, scarcely listening, went on, "In a novel, Katia's visit would be a real-estate tour. She would drive up from Biarritz with her mother and take pictures from the road. Katia's mother would find the house squat and suburban, and so Luc would show them Cousin Henri's. They would take pictures of that, too. Luc would now be going round with chalk and a tape measure, marking the furniture he wants to sell once we're buried, planning the rooms he will build for Katia when the place is his."

All at once he felt the thrust of the next generation, and for the first time he shared some of Simone's fear of the unknown girl.

"The house is yours," said Simone, mistaking his meaning. "The furniture is mine. They can't change that by going round with a piece of chalk. There's always the bank. She can't find *that* suburban." The bank had recently acquired a new and unexpected advantage: it was too small to be nationalized. "Your son is a dreamer," said Simone. "He dreams he is studying, and he fails his exams. He dreams about sex and revolutions, and he waits around for letters and listens to old men telling silly tales."

Roger remembered the hole drilled in the wall. An *au pair* girl in the shower was Luc's symbol of sexual mystery. From the great courtesans of his grandfather's time to the prettiest children of the poor in bordellos to a girl glimpsed as she stood drying herself—what a decline! Here was the true comedown, the real debasement of the middle class. Perhaps he would write a book about it; it would at least rival Mr. Brunt's opus about the decline of French officers.

"She can't spell," said Simone, examining the letter again. "If Luc marries her, he will have to write all her invitations and her postcards." What else did women write? She paused, wondering.

"Her journal?" Roger said.

In Cassandra's journal Simone read, "They expect such a lot from that poor clod of a Luc." That night at dinner Simone remarked, "My father once said he could die happy. He had never entertained a foreigner or shaken hands with an Englishman."

Cassandra stared at Roger as if to say, Is she joking? Roger, married twenty-three years, thought she was not. Cassandra's pale hair swung down as she drooped over her plate. She began to pick at something that, according to her diary, made her sick: underdone lamb, cooked the French way, stinking of garlic and spilling blood.

At dawn there was a spring thunderstorm, like the start of civil war. The gunfire died, and a hard, steady rain soaked the tennis court and lawn. Roger got up, first in the household, and let the dog out of the garage, where it slept among piles of paperbacks and rusting cans of weed killer. Roger was forty-eight that day; he hoped no one would notice. He thought he saw yellow roses running along the hedge, but it was a shaft of sunlight. In the kitchen, he found a pot with the remains of last night's coffee and heated some in a saucepan. While he drank, standing, looking out the window, the sky cleared entirely and became soft and blue.

"Happy birthday."

He turned his head, and there was Cassandra in the doorway, wearing a long gypsy skirt and an embroidered nightshirt, with toy rings on every finger. "I thought I'd dress because of

Sunday," she explained. "I thought we might be going to church."

"I could offer you better coffee in the village," said Roger. "If you do not mind the walk." He imagined her diary entry: "The Baron tried to get me alone on a country road, miles from any sign of habitation."

"The dog will come, too," he assured her.

They walked on the rim of wet fields, in which the freed dog leaped. The hem of Cassandra's skirt showed dark where it brushed against drenched grasses. Roger told her that the fields and woods, almost all they could see, had belonged to his grandparents. Cousin Henri owned the land now.

Cassandra knew; when Simone was not talking about Luc and Katia and the government, she talked about Cousin Henri.

"My father wants to write another book, about Torquemada and Stalin and, I think, Cromwell," Cassandra said. "The theme would be single-mindedness. But he can't get down to it. My mother doesn't see why he can't write for an hour, then talk to her for an hour. She asks him to help look for things she's lost, like the keys to the car. Before he retired, she was never bored. Now that he's home all day, she wants company and she loses everything."

"How did he write his other books?" said Roger.

"In the minstrel he had a private office and secretary. Two, in fact. He expected to write even more, once he was free, but he obviously won't. If he were alone, I could look after him." That was unexpected. Perhaps Luc knew just how unexpected Cassandra could be, and that was why he stayed away from her. "I don't mean I imagine my mother not there," she said. "I only meant that I could look after him, if I had to."

Half a mile before the village stood Cousin Henri's house. Roger told Cassandra why he and Henri were not speaking, except through lawyers. Henri had been grossly favored by their mutual grandparents, thanks to the trickery of an aunt by marriage, who was Henri's godmother. The aunt, who was very rich as well as mad and childless, had acquired the grandparents' domain, in their lifetime, by offering more money than it was worth. She had done this wicked thing in order to hand it over, intact, unshared, undivided, to Henri, whom she worshipped. The transaction had been brought off on the wrong side of the law, thanks to a clan of Protestants and Freemasons.

Cassandra looked puzzled and pained. "You see, the government of that time..." said Roger, but he fell silent, seeing that Cassandra had stopped understanding. When he was overwrought he sounded like his wife. It was hardly surprising: he was simply repeating, word for word, everything Simone had been saying since they were married. In his own voice, which was ironic and diffident, he told Cassandra why Cousin Henri had never married. At the age of twenty Henri had been made trustee of a family secret. Henri's mother was illegitimate—at any rate, hatched from a cuckoo's egg. Henri's father was not his mother's husband but a country neighbor. Henri had been warned never to marry any of the such-and-such girls, because he might be marrying his own half sister. Henri might not have wanted to: the such-and-suches were ugly and poor. He had used the secret as good reason not to marry anyone, had settled down in the handsomest house in the Yonne (half of which should have been Roger's), and had peopled the neighborhood with his random children.

They slowed walking, and Cassandra looked at a brick-and-stucco box, and some dirty-faced children playing on the steps.

"There, behind the farmhouse," said Roger, showing a dark, severe manor house at the top of a straight drive.

"It looks more like a monastery, don't you think?" said Cassandra. Although Roger seemed to be waiting, she could think of nothing more to say. They walked on, toward Cassandra's breakfast.

On the road back, Roger neither looked at Cousin Henri's house nor mentioned it. They were still at some distance from home when they began to hear Simone: "Marry her! Marry

Katia! Live with Katia! I don't care what you do. Anything, anything, so long as you pass your exam." Roger pushed open the gate and there was Simone, still in her dressing gown, standing on a lawn strewn with Luc's clothes, and Luc at the window, still in pajamas. Luc heaved a chair over the sill, then a couple of pillows and a whole armful of books. Having yelled something vile about the family (they were in disagreement later about what it was), he jumped out, too, and landed easily in a flower bed. He paused to pick up shoes he had flung out earlier, ran awkwardly across the lawn, pushed through a gap in the hedge, and vanished.

"He'll be back," said Simone, gathering books. "He'll want his breakfast. He really is a remarkable athlete. With proper guidance, Luc could have done anything. But Roger never took much interest."

"What was that last thing he said?" said Cassandra.

"Fools," said Simone. "But a common word for it. Never repeat that word, if you want people to think well of you."

"Spies," Roger had heard. In Luc's room he found a pair of sunglasses on the floor. He had noticed Luc limping as he made for the hedge; perhaps he had sprained an ankle. He remembered how Luc had been too tired to walk a dog, too worn out to feed a goldfish. Roger imagined him, now, wandering in muddy farmyards, in shoes and pajamas, children giggling at him—the Clairevoies' mooncalf son. Perhaps he had gone to tell his troubles to that other eccentric, Cousin Henri.

Tears came easily since Roger's last attack. He had been told they were caused by the depressant effect of the pills he had to take. He leaned on the window frame, in the hope of seeing Luc, and wept quietly in the shelter of Luc's glasses.

"It's awfully curious of me," said Cassandra, helping Simone, "but what's got into Luc? When he stayed with us, in England, he was angelic. Your husband seems upset, too."

"The *Baron*," said Simone, letting it be known she had read the diary and was ready for combat, "the *Baron* is too sensible. Today is his birthday. He is forty-eight—nearly fifty."

Roger supposed she meant "sensitive." To correct Simone might create a diversion, but he could not be sure of what kind. To let it stand might bewilder the English girl; but, then, Cassandra was born bewildered.

Luc came home in time for dinner, dressed in a shirt and corduroys belonging to Cousin Henri. His silence, Roger thought, challenged them for questions; none came. He accepted a portion of Roger's birthday cake, which, of course, Roger could not touch, and left half on his plate. "Even as a small child, Luc never cared for chocolate," Simone explained to Cassandra.

The next day, only food favored by Luc was served. Simone turned over a letter from Katia. It was brief and cool in tone: Katia had been exercising horses in a riding school, helping a friend.

The Clairevoies, preceded by Luc on the Honda, packed up and drove back to Paris. This time Cassandra was allowed to sit in front, next to Simone. Roger and the dog shared the back seat with Luc's books and a number of parcels.

They saw Cassandra off at the Gare du Nord. Roger was careful not to take her arm, brush against her, or otherwise inspire a mention in her diary. She wore a T-shirt decorated with a grinning mouth. "It's been really lovely," she said. Roger bowed.

Her letter of thanks arrived promptly. She was planning to help her father with his book on Stalin, Cromwell, and Torquemada. He wanted to include a woman on the list, to bring the work in line with trends of the day. Cassandra had suggested Boadicea, Queen of the Iceni. Boadicea stood for feminine rectitude, firmness, and true love of one's native culture. So Cassandra felt.

"Cassandra has written a most learned and affectionate letter," said Simone, who would never have to see Cassandra again. "I only hope Luc was as polite to the Brunts." Her voice held a new tone of maternal grievance and maternal threat.

Luc, who no longer found threats alarming, packed his books and took the train for Rennes. Katia's letters seemed to have stopped. Searching Luc's room, Simone found nothing to read except a paperback on private ownership. "I believe he is taking an interest in things," she told Roger.

It was late in May when the Clairevoies made their final trip to Rennes. Suspecting what awaited them, Simone wore mourning—a dark linen suit, black sandals, sunglasses. Father Rousseau had on a dark suit and black tie. After some hesitation he said what Roger was waiting to hear: it was useless to make Luc sit for an examination he had not even a remote chance of passing. Luc was unprepared, now and forever. He had, in fact, disappeared, though he had promised to come back once the talk with his parents was over. Luc had confided that he would be content to live like Cousin Henri, without a degree to his name, and with a reliable tenant farmer to keep things running.

My son is a fool, said Roger to himself. Katia, who was certainly beautiful, perhaps even clever, loved him. She stood crying in the street, trying to see a light in his room.

"Luc's cousin is rich," said Simone. "Luc is too pure to understand the difference. He will have to learn something. What about computer training?"

"Luc has a mind too fluid to be restrained," said Father Rousseau.

"Literature?" said Simone, bringing up the last resort.

Roger came to life. "Sorting letters in the post office?"

"Machines do that," said Father Rousseau. "Luc would have to pass a test to show he understands the machine. I have been wondering if there might be in Luc's close environment a family affair." The Clairevoies fell silent. "A family business," Father

Rousseau repeated. "Families are open, airy structures. They take in the dreamy as well as the alert. There is always an extra corner somewhere."

Like most of her women friends, Simone had given up wearing jewelry: the streets were full of anarchists and muggers. One of her friends knew of someone who had had a string of pearls ripped off her neck by a bearded intellectual of the Mediterranean type—that is, quite dark. Simone still kept, for luck, a pair of gold earrings, so large and heavy they looked fake. She touched her talisman earrings and said, "We have in our family a bank too small to be nationalized."

"Congratulations," said Father Rousseau, sincerely. When he got up to see them to the door, Roger saw he wore running shoes.

It fell to Roger to tell Luc what was to become of him. After military service of the most humdrum and unprotected kind, he would move to a provincial town and learn about banks. The conversation took place late one night in Luc's room. Simone had persuaded Roger that Luc needed to be among his own things—the galleon lamp, the Foreign Legion recruiting poster that had replaced Che Guevara, the photograph of Simone that replaced Roger's graduating class. Roger said, somewhat shyly, "You will be that much closer to Biarritz."

"Katia is getting married," said Luc. "His father has a riding school." He said this looking away, rolling a pencil between thumb and finger, something like the way his mother had rolled a kitchen match. Reflected in the dark window, Luc's cheeks were hollowed, his eyes blazing and black. He looked almost a hero and, like most heroes, lonely.

"What happened to your friends?" said Roger. "The friends you used to see every Sunday."

"Oh, that...that fell apart. All the people they ever talked about were already dead. And some of the parents were worried. You were the only parents who never interfered."

"We wanted you to live your own life," said Roger. "It must have been that. Could you get her back?"

"You can do anything with a woman if you give her enough money."

"Who told you a thing like that?" In the window Roger examined the reflected lamp, the very sight of which was supposed to have made a man of Luc.

"Everyone. Cousin Henri. I told her we owned a bank, because Cousin Henri said it would be a good thing to tell her. She asked me how to go about getting a bank loan. That was all."

Does he really believe he owns a bank, Roger wondered. "About money," he said. "Nothing of Cousin Henri's is likely to be ours. Illegitimate children are allowed to inherit now, and my cousin," said Roger with some wonder, "has acknowledged everyone. I pity the schoolteacher. All she ever sees is the same face." This was not what Luc was waiting to hear. "You will inherit everything your mother owns. I have to share with my cousin, because that is how our grandparents arranged it." He did not go on about the Freemasons and Protestants, because Luc already knew.

"It isn't fair," said Luc.

"Then you and your mother share my share."

"How much of yours is mine?" said Luc politely.

"Oh, something at least the size of the tennis court," said Roger.

On Luc's desk stood, silver-framed, another picture of Simone, a charming one taken at the time of her engagement. She wore, already, the gold earrings. Her hair was in the upswept balloon style of the time. Her expression was smiling, confident but untried. Both Luc and Roger suddenly looked at it in silence.

It was Simone's belief that, after Katia, Luc had started sleeping with one of her own friends. She thought she knew the one: the Hungarian wife of an architect, fond of saying she wished she had a daughter the right age for Luc. This was a direct sexual compliment, based on experience, Simone thought. Roger thought it meant nothing at all. It was the kind of empty declaration mothers mistook for appreciation. Simone had asked

Roger to find out what he could, for this was the last chance either of them would ever have to talk to Luc. From now on, he would undoubtedly get along better with his parents, but where there had been a fence there would be a wall. Luc was on his own.

Roger said, "It was often thought, in my day, mainly by foreigners who had never been to France, that young men began their lives with their mother's best friend. Absurd, when you consider it. Why pick an old woman when you can have a young one?" *Buy* a young one, he had been about to say, by mistake. "Your mother's friends often seem young to me. I suppose it has to do with their clothes—so loose, unbuttoned. The disorder is already there. My mother's best friends wore armor. It was called the New Look, invented by Christian Dior, a great defender of matronly virtue." A direct glance from Luc—the first. "There really was a Mr. Dior, just as I suppose there was a Mr. Mercedes and a Mr. Benz. My mother and her friends were put into boned corsets, stiff petticoats, wide-brimmed, murderous hats. Their nails were pointed, and as red as your lampshade. They carried furled parasols with silver handles and metal-edged handbags. Even the heels of their shoes were contrived for braining people. No young man would have gone anywhere near." Luc's eyes met Roger's in the window. "I have often wondered," said Roger, "though I'm not trying to make it my business, what you and Katia could have done. Where could you have taken her? Well, unless she had some private place of her own. There's more and more of that. Daughters of nice couples, people we know. Their own apartment, car, money. Holidays no one knows where. Credit cards, bank accounts, abortions. In my day, we had a miserable amount of spending money, but we had the girls in the Rue Spontini. Long after the bordellos were closed, there was the Rue Spontini. Do you know who first took me there? Cousin Henri. Not surprising, considering the life he has led since. Henri called it 'the annex,' because he ran into so many friends from his school. On Thursday afternoons, that was." A slight

question in Luc's eyes. "Thursday was our weekly holiday, like
Wednesdays for you. I don't suppose every Wednesday—no, I'm
sure you don't. Besides, even the last of those places vanished
years ago. There were Belgian girls, Spanish girls from Algeria.
Some were so young—oh, very young. One told me I was like a
brother. I asked Cousin Henri what she meant. He said he didn't
know."

Luc said, "Katia could cry whenever she wanted to." Her face
never altered, but two great tears would suddenly brim over and
course along her cheeks.

The curtains and shutters were open. Anyone could look in.
There was no one in the street—not even a ghost. How real Katia
and Luc had seemed; how they had touched what was left of
Roger's heart; how he had loved them. Giving them up forever,
he said, "I always admired that picture of your mother."

Simone and Roger had become engaged while Roger was still
a lieutenant in Algeria. On the night before their wedding, which
was to take place at ten o'clock in the morning in the church of
Saint-Pierre de Chaillot, Roger paid a wholly unwelcome call.
Simone received him alone, in her dressing gown, wearing a fine
net over her carefully ballooned hair. Her parents, listening at the
door, took it for granted Roger had caught a venereal disease in a
North African brothel and wanted the wedding postponed;
Simone supposed he had met a richer and prettier girl. All Roger
had to say was that he had seen an Algerian prisoner being
tortured to death. Simone had often asked Roger, since then,
why he had tried to frighten her with something that had so little
bearing on their future. Roger could not remember what his
reason had been.

He tried, now, to think of something important to say to Luc,
as if the essence of his own life could be bottled in words and
handed over. Sylvestre, wakened by a familiar voice, came
snuffling at the door, expecting at this unsuitable hour to be taken
out. Roger remarked, "Whatever happens, don't get your life all
mixed up with a dog's."

A PAINFUL AFFAIR

Grippes' opinion remains unchanged: He was the last author to have received a stipend from the Mary Margaret Pugh Arts Foundation, and so it should have fallen to him—Henri Grippes, Parisian novelist, diarist, essayist, polemical journalist, and critic—to preside at the commemoration of the late Miss Pugh's centenary. (This celebration, widely reported in Paris, particularly in publications that seemed to have it in for Grippes, took place in a room lent by the firm of Fronce & Baril, formerly drapers and upholsterers, now purveyors of bluejeans from Madras. The firm's books reveal that Miss Pugh was the first person ever to have opened a charge account—a habit she brought from her native America and is thought to have introduced into France.) But the honor did not fall to M. Grippes. The Pugh Memorial Committee, made up of old-age pensioners from the American Embassy, the Chase Manhattan Bank (Paris), the French Ministry for Culture, and other intellectual oatcakes, chose instead to invite Victor Prism, winkling him with no trouble out of his obscure post at a university in the North of England. Prism's eagerness to get away from England whatever the season, his willingness to travel under foul conditions, for a trifling sum of money, make him a popular feature of subsidized gatherings throughout the Free World. This is still the way Grippes sees things.

Prism, author of *Suomi Serenade: A Key to the Kalevala*, much praised in its day as an outstandingly skillful performance, also thinks Grippes should have been chairman. The fact that the Pugh centenary celebration coincided with the breakup of the M. M. Pugh Investment Trust, from which the Foundation—and, incidentally, M. Grippes—had drawn considerable funds over the years, might have made Grippes' presence in the chair especially poignant. It could also have tested his capacity for showing humility—an accommodation already strained more than once. Think of Grippes, Miss Pugh's youthful protégé, fresh from his father's hog farm in Auvergne, dozing on a bed in her house (a bed that had belonged to Prism a scant six months before), with Rosalia, the maid, sent along every half hour to see how he was getting on with Chapter 2. Think of Grippes at the end, when Miss Pugh's long-lost baby brother, now seventy-something—snappy Hong Kong forty-eight-hour tailoring, silk shirt from Bangkok, arrogant suntan—turned up at her bedside, saying, "Well, Maggie, long time no see."

"She died in his arms," wrote Grippes, in an unusually confidential letter to Prism, "though not without a struggle."

Prism says he had been promised Miss Pugh's library, her collection of autograph letters (Apollinaire to Zola), her matching ormolu-mounted opaline urns, her Meissen coffee service, her father's cufflinks, her Louis XVI period writing table, and the key to a safe-deposit vault containing two Caillebottes and a Morisot. The promise was not kept, but no trick of fortune could possibly erode his gratitude for earlier favors. He still visits Miss Pugh's grave, in a mossy corner of Passy Cemetery, whenever he happens to be in Paris. He leaves a bunch of anemones, or a pot of chrysanthemums, or, when the cost of flowers is really sky-high, merely stands silently with his head bowed. Sunshine flows upon the back of his neck, in a kind of benison. Seeing how the rich are buried imbues him with strengthened faith. He receives the formal promise of a future offered and accepted—a pledge he once believed existed in art. He thinks of Grippes, in his flat across the Seine, scribbling away amid Miss Pugh's furniture and his tribe of stray cats.

Grippes says he visits Miss Pugh's grave as often as he is able. (He has to find someone to stay with the cats.) Each time he goes to the cemetery he gets caught up in a phalanx of mourners shuffling behind a creeping hearse. The hearse parks close to some family mausoleum that is an architectural echo of the mansions that lined Avenue du Bois before it became Avenue Foch. Waiting for the coffin to be unloaded, the mourners stare at one another's collars. Grippes reads inscriptions on tombstones, some of which indicate with astonishing precision what the occupant expected to find on the other side. In this place, where it is never spring, he is conscious of bare branches, dark birds cawing. The day takes on a grainy texture, like a German Expressionist film. The only color glows from the ribbons and rosettes some of the mourners wear on their lapels. (Among the crumbs flicked in Grippes' direction was Miss Pugh's Legion of Honor, after her brother had been assured it would not fetch one franc, his floor price, at auction.) There is nothing extravagant or dangerous about these excursions. They cost Grippes a Métro ticket each way—direct line, Montparnasse-Trocadéro, no awkward change, no transfer, no flight along underground corridors pursued by a gang of those savage children of whom even the police are afraid.

Prism thinks that Grippes started showing signs of infantile avarice and timidity soon after Miss Pugh's death, which left him homeless. For a time Grippes even thought of moving to London. He sent Prism a letter suggesting they take a flat together and live on their memories. Prism responded with a strange and terrifying account of gang wars, with pimps and blackmailers shot dead on the steps of the National Gallery. In

Paris, Prism wrote, Grippes could be recognized on sight as a literary odd-jobs man with style. No one would call him a climber—at least, not to his face. Rather, Grippes seemed to have been dropped in early youth onto one of those middling-high peaks of Paris bohemia from which the artist can see both machine-knit and cashmere blazers hanging in Boulevard Haussmann department stores and five-thousand-franc custom tailoring. In England, where caste signs were radically different, he might give the false impression that he was a procurer or a drug pusher and be gunned down at a bus stop.

After reading this letter, Grippes got out a map of London and studied it. It looked crowded and untidy. He cashed in about half the bonds Miss Pugh had made over to him in her lifetime and bought four rooms above a cinema in Montparnasse. While he was showing the removal men where to place Miss Pugh's writing table, a cat came mewing at the door and he let it in.

Grippes denies the imputation of avarice. When Prism gave his famous lecture in Brussels, in 1970, "Is Language a Deterrent?," Grippes travelled by train to hear him, at his own expense. He recalls that Prism was wearing a green corduroy suit, a canary-yellow V-neck sweater, and a tie that must have been a souvenir of Belfast. On his return to Paris, Grippes wrote a lighthearted essay about *le style Anglais*.

Just before the centennial, Prism was interviewed on French television: eighteen minutes of Victor Prism, at a green baize table, with an adulating journalist who seemed to have been dipped in shellac. Prism's French had not deteriorated, though it still sounded to Grippes like dried peas rattling in a tin can. "The fact is," he said, rattling, "that I am the only person who knew Miss Pugh well—apart from her devoted servant Rosalia, that is. All raise hands, please, who remember Rosalia. (*Camera on studio smiles*) I am the person who called on Miss Pugh after she was evicted from her beautiful house and transported by ambulance to a nursing home in Meudon. She never quite understood that she had bought a house but not the land it stood on. (*Sympathetic laughter*) The last time I saw her, she was sitting up in bed, wearing her sapphire earrings, drinking a bottle of Veuve Clicquot. I have forgotten to say that she was by now completely bald, which did not make her in the least self-conscious. (*Immense good will*) I was obliged to return to England, believing I was leaving Miss Pugh in radiant health and in trusted hands." (*Audience delight*)

A heavily edited version of Grippes' answer appeared in *Le Figaro*, under the heading "A Painful Affair: Further Correspondence." Mr. Prism had neglected to mention the date of Miss Pugh's transfer to the nursing home: 10 May, 1968. Clouds of tear gas. Cars overturned in Paris streets. Grippes' long-awaited autobiographical novel, *Sleeping on the Beach*, had appeared the day before. His stoic gloom as he watched students flinging the whole of the first edition onto a bonfire blazing as high as second-story windows. Grippes' publisher, crouched in his shabby office just around the corner, had already hung on the wall the photograph of some hairy author he hoped would pass for Engels. The glow from the bonfire tinged bogus Engels pink, investing him with the hearty tone that had quit the publisher's cheeks when, early that morning, a delegation representing what might well turn out to be a New Order had invaded the premises. Grippes, pale trenchcoat over dark turtleneck, hands clenched in trenchcoat pockets, knew he was aging, irreversibly, minute by minute. Some of the students thought he was Herbert Marcuse and tried to carry him on their shoulders to *Le Figaro*'s editorial offices, which they hoped he would set on fire. The melancholia that descended on Grippes that evening made him unfit to help and sustain an old lady who was said to be spending all her time sulking under a bedsheet and refusing to eat. He managed to be with Miss Pugh at the end, however, and distinctly heard her say something coherent about the disposal of her furniture. As for *Sleeping on the Beach*, it was never reprinted, for the usual craven reasons.

Prism says that even before the Pugh Investment Trust filed its bankruptcy petition before a Paris court, the dismantling of Miss Pugh's house had been completed, with the wainscoting on the staircase stripped and sold to a tearoom and what remained of the silver, pictures, and furniture brought under the hammer. (Grippes and Rosalia had already removed some of the better pieces, for safety.) Her will was so ambiguous that, to avoid litigation, Miss Pugh's brother and the Trust split the proceeds, leaving Prism and a few other faithful friends of hers in the cold. Grippes is suspected of having gold ingots under the bed, bullion in the bathtub, gold napoleons in his shoes. The fact is (Grippes can prove it) that Miss Pugh's personal income had been declining for years, owing to her steadfast belief that travel by steamship would soon supersede the rage for planes. "Her private investments followed her convictions as night follows day," writes Grippes, with the cats for company. "And, one day, night fell."

Prism discovered that some of the furniture removed for safety was in the parlor of Rosalia's son, permanent mayor and Mafia delegate of a town in Sicily. He at once dispatched an expert appraiser, who declared the whole lot to be fake. It may have been that on a pink marble floor, against pink wall hangings, in a room containing a bar on which clockwork figures of Bonaparte and Josephine could be made to play Ping-Pong, Miss Pugh's effects took on an aura of sham. Still, the expert seemed sincere to Prism. He said the Boulle chest was the kind they still manufacture on the Rue du Faubourg Saint-Martin, scar with bleach, beat with chains, then spend years restoring.

About a month after the funeral, a letter appeared in *Le Matin de Paris*, signed "Old-Style Socialist." The writer recalled that some forty years before, a Miss Pugh (correctly spelled) had purchased from an antique dealer a wooden statue said to represent St. Cumula, virgin and martyr. (A brief history of Cumula followed: about to be forced into marriage with a pagan

Gaul, Cumula painted herself purple and jumped into the Seine, where she drowned. The pagan, touched by her unwavering detestation of him, accepted Christian baptism, on the site of what is now the Paris Stock Exchange.) Miss Pugh had the effigy restored to its original purple and offered it to the Archbishop of Paris. After several coats of paint were removed, the carving was found to be a likeness of General Marchand, leader of the French Nile Expedition. The Archbishop declined the present, giving as his reason the separation of church and state. "Old-Style Socialist" wondered what had become of the carving, for even if General Marchand stood for nineteenth-century colonial policy at its most offensive, history was history, art was art, and it was easily proved that some persons never ceased to meddle in both.

Prism believes Grippes might have had some talent to begin with but that he wasted it writing tomfool letters. He thinks a note that came in the mail recently was from Grippes: "Dear Ms. Victoria Prism, I teach Creative Journalism to a trilingual class here in California (Spanish/Chinese/some English). In the past you have written a lot of stuff that was funny and made us laugh. Lately you published something about the lingering death of a helicopter pilot. Is this a new departure? Please limit your answer to 200 words. My class gets tired." The letter had an American stamp and a Los Angeles postmark, but Prism has known Grippes to spend days over such details.

Grippes says that Prism's talent is like one of those toy engines made of plastic glass, every part transparent and moving to no purpose. The engine can be plugged in to a power outlet, but it can't be harnessed. In short, Prism symbolizes the state of English letters since the nineteen-fifties.

"You ought to write your memoirs," Grippes said to Prism at Miss Pugh's funeral. Prism thought Grippes was hoping to be provided with grounds for a successful libel action. (He concedes that Grippes looked fine that day: dark tie, dark suit, well brushed—he hadn't begun collecting cats yet.)

Actually, Prism is pretty sure he could fill two volumes, four hundred pages each, dark-green covers, nice paper, nice to touch. A title he has in mind is *Bridge Building Between Cultures*.

Grippes started his own memoirs about a year ago, basing them on his diaries. He wouldn't turn down a Bibliothèque de la Pléiade edition, about a thousand pages of Bible-weight paper, fifty pages of pictures, full Grippes bibliography, appreciative introductory essay by someone he has not quarrelled with, frontispiece of Grippes at the window, back to the light, three-quarter profile, cat on his shoulder. He'd need pictures of Miss Pugh: there are none. She loathed sitting for portraits, photographs, snapshots. Old prints of her house exist, their negatives lost or chewed by mice. The Pugh Memorial Committee donated a few to the Museum of Popular Arts and Traditions, where they were immediately filed under "Puget, Pierre, French sculptor."

"Research might have better luck at the University of Zurich," writes Grippes, at Miss Pugh's Louis XVI period table. "A tireless Swiss team has been on the trail of Miss Pugh for some time now, and a cowed Swiss computer throws up only occasional anarchy, describing Pugh M. M., Pullman G. M., and Pulitzer J. as the same generous American."

Prism's quiet collaboration with Zurich, expected to culminate in a top-quality volume, *Hostess to Fame*, beige linen cover, ended when he understood that he was not going to be paid anything, and that it would be fifteen years before the first word was transferred from tape to paper.

Grippes says he heard one of the tapes:

"Mr. Prism, kindly listen to the name I shall now pronounce. François Mauriac. The thin, sardonic gentleman who put on a bowler hat every morning before proceeding to Mass was François Mauriac. Right?"

"I don't remember a François."

"Think. François. Mauriac."

"I don't remember a bowler hat."

At the centennial commemoration, Prism stood on a little dais, dressed in a great amount of tweed and flannel that seemed to have been cut for a much larger man. Grippes suspects that Prism's clothes are being selected by his widowed sister, who, after years of trying to marry him off to her closest friends, is now hoping to make him seem as unattractive as possible. Imagining Prism's future—a cottage in Devon, his sister saying, "There was a letter for you, but I can't remember what I did with it"—he heard Prism declare he was happy to be here, in a place obligingly provided; the firm's old boardroom, back in the days when Paris was still; the really fine walnut panelling on two of the; about the shortage of chairs, but the Committee had not expected such a large; some doubtless disturbed by an inexplicable smell of moth repellent, but the Committee was in no way; in honor of a great and charitable American, to whom the cultural life of; looking around, he was pleased to see one or two young faces.

With this, Prism stepped down, and had to be reminded he was chairman and principal speaker. He climbed back, and delivered from memory an old lecture of his on Gertrude Stein. He then found and read a letter Miss Pugh had received from the President of the Republic, in 1934, telling her that although she was a woman, and a foreigner, she was surely immortal. Folding the letter, Prism suddenly recalled and described a conversation with Miss Pugh.

"Those of us who believe in art," Prism had started to say.
Miss Pugh had coughed and said, "I don't."

She did not believe in art, only in artists. She had no interest in books, only in their authors. Reading an early poem of Prism's (it was years since he had written any poetry, he hastened to say), she had been stopped by the description of a certain kind of butterfly, "pale yellow, with a spot like the Eye of God." She had sent for her copy of the Larousse dictionary, which Rosalia was using in the kitchen as a weight on sliced cucumbers. Turning to a color plate, Miss Pugh had found the butterfly at once. It turned out to be orange rather than yellow, and heavily spotted with black. Moreover, it was not a European butterfly but an Asian moth. The Larousse must be mistaken. She had shut the dictionary with a slap, blaming its editors for carelessness. If only there had been more women like her, Prism concluded, there would be more people today who knew what they were doing.

Grippes says that, for once, he feels inclined to agree. All the same, he wishes Prism had suppressed the anecdote. Prism knows as well as Grippes does that some things are better left as legends.

LARRY

Some men give their children sound advice about property and investment. The elder Pugh had the nerve to give advice about marriage—this to the son of a wife he had deserted. He was in Paris on a visit and had come round to see what Larry was up to. It was during the hot, quiet summer of 1954.

Larry was caretaking for July and August. He had the run of sixteen dust-sheeted rooms, some overlooking the Parc de Monceau, some looking straight onto the shuttered windows of other stone houses. Twice a week a woman arrived to clean and, Larry supposed, to make sure he hadn't stolen anything.

He was not a thief—only a planner. His plans required the knowledge of where things were kept and what they amounted to. After a false start as a sculptor he was trying to find an open road. He went through the drawers and closets left unlocked and came across a number of towels and bathmats and blankets stolen from hotels; pilfering of that sort was one of the perks of the rich. A stack of hotel writing paper gave him a new idea for teasing

Maggie, his half sister, who also lived in Paris—near the
Trocadéro, about eight Métro stops away.

The distance between Larry and Maggie was greater than any
stretch of city blocks. He saw it as a treeless plain. It was she who
kept the terrain bare, so that she could see Larry coming. He had
to surmise, because it would be senseless to do anything else, that
Maggie failed to trust him. He wondered why. Total strangers,
with even more reason to feel suspicious, gave him the keys to
their house. When he looked in a mirror, he felt he could trust
himself. A French law obliges children to support indigent
parents and, in one or two rare cases Larry had heard of,
siblings—a sister or brother. Maggie probably lived with the fear
of seeing Larry shuffling up to the front door, palm up. Or
carrying a briefcase stuffed with claims and final warnings. Or
ringing the bell, in a tearing hurry, with a lawyer waiting in a taxi.
Or that she would be called to his bedside at the American
Hospital in Neuilly, with an itemized statement for intensive care
prepared at checkout. She might even be afraid she would have
to bury him, in the unlikely event of his dying first. Maggie's
mother, but not Larry's, had been crowningly rich. Larry's
generation would have said that he and Maggie had different
genes; Maggie's would have taken it for granted they had
different prospects.

Fiddling around with the hotel stationery, he sent Maggie
letters from Le Palais in Biarritz, the Hôtel de Paris in Monte
Carlo, Le Royal at Évian-les-Bains, Le Golf at Deauville. Some
carried the terrifying P.S. "See you soon!" From the Paris Ritz
he counselled her not to mind the number of bills he was having
referred to her from Biarritz and those other places: he had made
a killing in Portuguese oysters and would settle up with her
before long.

He wondered if the tease had worked, and if she had bothered
to look at the postmarks. He had sent all the letters from the same
post office, on Boulevard Malesherbes. The postmarks should
have shown Maggie that it was just a prank, not an operation. But
then she probably thought him too old for practical jokes and

wholly unsuited for operations. A true trickster needed to have
the elder Pugh's clear conscience—his perfect innocence.

Paris was hushed, eerie, Larry's father said. That was what he
noticed after so many years. He'd gone back to America long
before the war. For some time now Maggie had been paying him
an allowance to keep away. She lived in Paris because she always
had; it did not mean that she kept open house. Larry was here for
a different reason: he had been at the Beaux Arts for as long as he
could stretch the G.I. Bill. He was just wavering at present: stay
or go.

He told his father why Paris was silent. There was a new law
about traffic horns. His father said he didn't believe it.

Here, near the park, in midsummer, there was no traffic to
speak of. In the still of the afternoon they heard the braking of a
bus across the empty streets. Shutters were bolted, curtains
drawn on the streets with art names: Murillo, Rembrandt, Van
Dyck.

Larry's father said, "I suppose you found out there wasn't
much to art in the long run." From anyone else it would have
been wounding. His father meant only that there were better
things in life, not that anyone had failed him.

Larry took the dust sheets off an inlaid table and two pink easy
chairs. The liquor cabinet was easy to pry open; he managed with
a fork and spoon. They pushed their chairs over to a window. It
was curious, his father remarked, how the French never wanted
to look *out*. Notice the way salon furniture is placed—those stiff
little circles. People always sat as if they weren't sure what to do
with their ankles and knees.

The drawing room was pale in color, and yet it soaked up the
light. Larry was about to ask if his father had ever seen a total
eclipse, when the old man said, "Who lives around here? It was a
good address before the war."

Before the other war, he meant—before 1914. He was fine-
looking—high-bridged nose, only slightly veined; tough, kindly
blue eyes. He seemed brainless to Larry, like Maggie, but a
stranger might not have noticed. His gaze was alert as a wren's,

his expression one of narrow sincerity. If there were such a thing as artistic truth, his face would have been more ingratiating; about half his plots and schemes had always died on the branch. He must have seen the other half as enough. Unlike most con men, Larry's father acted on sudden inclinations. It was a wonder anything bloomed at all.

Larry did not think of himself as brainless. He did not even consider himself unlucky, which proved he was smart. He was not sure whether his face said anything useful. It was almost too late to decide. He had stopped being young.

His father had no real age; certainly none in his own mind. He sat, comfortable and alert, drinking Larry's patron's best Scotch, telling Larry about a wonderful young woman who was dying to marry him. But, he said, probably having quite correctly guessed that Maggie would cut his funds at the very glimmer of a new wedding, he thought he'd keep the dew on the rose; stick to untrammelled romance; maintain the constant delight and astonishment reserved for unattached lovers. She was attractive, warmhearted, and intelligent; made all her own clothes.

Larry refrained from asking questions, partly out of loyalty to his late, put-upon mother. Dead or alive, she had heard enough. "Marriage is sex," said his father. "But money is not necessarily anything along that line." In spite of his wish not to be drawn, Larry could not help mulling this over. His father was always at his most dangerous, morally speaking, when he made no sense. "The richer she is, the lower the class of her lovers. If you marry a rich woman, keep an eye on the chauffeur. Watch out for unemployed actors, sailors, tailors. *Customs* officers," he said, as though suddenly remembering. He may have been recalling Maggie's mother. He sighed, though not out of discontent or sorrow, and lifted his firm blue gaze to an oil portrait of a woman wearing pearls Maggie's mother would have swum the Amazon for. "I was never really excited by rich women," he said calmly. "Actually, I think only homosexuals are. Well, it is all a part of God's good plan, laid out for our pleasure, like the flower beds down there in the park."

Larry's father was a pagan who regularly prayed for guidance. He thought nothing of summoning God to smile on His unenlightened creations. Maggie, another object of close celestial attention, believed something should be done about the nature of the universe—some tidying-up job. She was ready to take it on and was only waiting to be asked. Larry lived at about eye level. He tried the Catholics, who said, "What would you like? Jam for breakfast? Eternal life? They're yours, but there's a catch." The Protestants greeted his return with "Shut up. Sit down. Think it over." It was like swimming back and forth between two crowded rafts.

"I met *your* mother just before I lost most of my money," his father said, which was a whitewashed way of explaining he had been involved in a mining-stock scandal of great proportions. "Never make the mistake of imagining a dumb woman is going to be more restful than a smart one. Most men crack up on that. They think 'dumb' means 'silent.' They think it's going to be like the baaing of a lamb and the cooing of a dove, and they won't need to answer. But soon it's 'Do you still love me?,' and that can't be left in the air. Then it turns into 'Did you love me when we got married? Did you love me when I was pregnant? Did you love me last week? Do you love me now?' "

Larry said, "I saw Maggie about a year ago. She says she's leaving everything to an arts foundation."

"She can't," said his father.

"She thinks she can, and she's got lawyers. It's her way of wanting to be remembered. But it's the wrong way. The French never remember anything except their own wars. She won't even have her name on a birdbath."

"Now, that's where you're wrong," his father said. "There'll be a memorial birdbath and Maggie's name—which, incidentally is yours and mine; I'm leaving you both a good name—and in the bowl of the birdbath there'll be the Stars and Stripes in red-white-and-blue mosaic. That is exactly what they'll give Maggie's memory. Where they will choose to put the monument I can't predict. No sane man wants to survive his own children, so I won't say I'd like to see the inaugural ceremony. You'll be there, though—well dressed and smiling. Life has been good to me. I hope it's just as good to you."

It was true that life had treated the old man gently; it had kept him out of jail and in cheerful company.

"I haven't made a formal will yet," he said, quite as though he had anything to leave. "But there's one particular thing I want *you* to have. It's a painting of me. I sat for it here, in Paris, before the war. Around 1912. I don't remember the artist's name, but he was big in those days. If you ever have a son, I want him to have the picture. Promise me you'll come and get it no matter where you happen to be when I go."

He helped himself to a drink and, as though no answer from Larry were needed, began to talk about something else he owned—an ancient hookah, a museum piece. Maggie would appreciate having it, he thought.

Larry noticed that their drinks were leaving rings on the inlaid table. He rubbed them with a corner of a dust sheet, but it was too late.

The next day, while he was trying to sandpaper the stains, Larry remembered the portrait. It showed his father wearing a hat at a jaunty angle, his hands clasped on a walking stick. He appeared to be elegant and reliable, the way things and people are always said to have been when one looks back at them across a war.

When Larry's father left Larry and his mother, he took the portrait with him. It must have been hanging in a dining room, because Larry saw him taking it down, and then tossing a bundle of money, cash, on a polished table. His mother sat in profile, turned away, arms folded. She looked toward, but not at, the little glass shelves at the window, where she kept her collection of miniature cacti in pottery dishes. She wore the look of dark grieving no child can enter. When he saw that she was not going to turn back his way or say something to him, Larry's father secured the portrait under his arm and walked out. There was a blank place on the wall, and on the table, deeply reflected, a packet of bills that seemed a lot but that never was or could be enough.

Over the next few days and until the end of August, when it was time for Larry to move on, he continued to work on the inlaid table, repeating the operation of sandpaper and wax until the rings showed but palely, and only under direct, strong light. Except for those faint circles, and a few sheets of hotel stationery and a few ounces of whiskey gone, he left no other trace behind him of loss or mischief.

A FLYING START

The project for a three-volume dictionary of literary biography, *Living Authors of the Fourth Republic*, was set afloat in Paris in 1952, with an eleven-man editorial committee in the same lifeboat. The young and promising Henri Grippes, spokesman for a new and impertinent generation, waited on shore for news of mass drownings; so he says now. A few years later, when the working title had to be changed to *Living Authors of the Fifth Republic*, Grippes was invited aboard. In 1964, Grippes announced there were not enough living authors to fill three volumes, and was heaved over the side. Actually, he had just accepted a post as writer-in-residence at a women's college in California; from the Pacific shore he sent a number of open letters to Paris weeklies, denouncing the dictionary scheme as an attempt to establish a form of literary pecking order. Anti-élitism was in the air, and Grippes' views received great prominence. His return to Paris found a new conflict raging: *two* volumes were now to be produced, under the brusque and fashionable title *Contemporary Writers, Women and Others*. Grippes at once published a pamphlet revealing that

118

it was a police dodge for feeding women and others into a multinational computer. In the event of invasion, the computer would cough up the names and the authors would be lined up and marched to forced labor in insurance companies. He carried the day, and for a time the idea of any contemporary literary directory was dropped.

Grippes had by then come into a little money, and had bought himself an apartment over a cinema in Montparnasse. He wore a wide felt hat and a velvet jacket in cool weather and a panama straw and a linen coat when it was fine. Instead of a shopping bag he carried a briefcase. He wrote to the mayor of Paris—who answered, calling him "Maître"—to protest a plan to remove the statue of Balzac from Boulevard Raspail, just north of the Boulevard du Montparnasse intersection. It was true that the statue was hemmed in by cars illegally parked and that it was defiled by pigeons, but Grippes was used to seeing it there. He also deplored that the clock on the corner near the Dôme no longer kept time; Grippes meant by this that it did not keep the same time as his watch, which he often forgot to wind.

In the meantime the old two-volume project, with its aging and dwindled editorial committee and its cargo of card-index files, had floated toward a reliable firm that published old-fashioned history manuals with plenty of color plates, and geography books that drew attention only to territories that were not under dispute. The Ministry of Culture was thought to be behind the venture. The files, no one quite knew how, were pried away from the committee and confided to a professor of English literature at a provincial university. The *Angliciste* would be unlikely to favor one school of French writing over another, for the simple reason that he did not know one from the other. The original committee had known a great deal, which was why for some thirty years its members had been in continual deadlock.

It seemed to the *Angliciste* that the work would have wider appeal if a section was included on British writers known for their slavish cultural allegiance to France. First on the list was, of

course, Victor Prism, lifelong and distinguished Francophile and
an old academic acquaintance. He recalled that Prism had once
lived in Paris as the protégé of Miss Mary Margaret Pugh, a
patroness of the arts; so, at about the same time, had the future
novelist and critic Henri Grippes. "Two golden lion cubs in the
golden cage of the great lioness," as the *Angliciste* wrote
Grippes, asking him to contribute a concise appreciation of his
comrade in early youth. "Just say what semed to you to be
prophetic of his achievement. We are in a great hurry. The work
is now called *French Authors, 1950–2000*, and we must go to
press by 1990 if it is to have any meaning for our time. Don't
trouble about Prism's career; the facts are on record. Payment
upon receipt of contribution, alas. The Ministry is being firm."

Grippes received the letter a week before Christmas. He
thought of sending Prism a sixteen-page questionnaire but
decided, reasonably, that it might dull the effect of surprise. He
set to work, and by dint of constant application completed his
memoir the following Easter. It was handwritten, of course; even
his sojourn in California had not reconciled Grippes to typewriters. "I feel certain this is what you are after," he wrote the
Angliciste. "A portrait of Prism as protégé. It was an experience
that changed his external image. Miss Pugh often said he had
arrived on her doorstep looking as if he had spent his life in the
rain waiting for a London bus. By the time he left, a few weeks
later, a wholehearted commitment to the popular Parisian idols
of the period—Sartre, Camus, and Charles Trenet—caused him
to wear a little gray hat with turned-up brim, a black shirt, an off-
white tie, and voluminous trousers. At his request, Miss Pugh
gave him a farewell present of crêpe-soled shoes. Perhaps, with
luck, you may find a picture of him so attired."

G rippes' memoir was untitled.
    " 'The drawing room at the Duchess of B——'s over-
looked a leafy avenue and a rustic bandstand in the city of O——.

There, summer after summer, the Duchess had watched children rolling their hoops to the strains of a polka, or a waltz, or a mazurka, or a sparkling military march, remote indeed from the harsh sound of warfare that assailed her today.'

"Would anyone believe, now, that Victor Prism could have written this? That Prism could have poured out, even once, the old bourgeois caramel sauce?

"He did. The time was soon after the end of the Second World War. They were the first words of his first unfinished novel, and they so impressed Miss Mary Margaret Pugh, an American lady then living in a bosky, sunless, and costly corner of Paris, that she invited Prism to complete the novel in her house.

"His benefactress, if extant, would be well over a hundred. In his unpublished roman à clef, *Goldfinches Have Yellow Feathers*, Prism left a picture of Miss Pugh he may still consider fair: 'Miss Melbourne, from a distance, reminded Christopher of those statues of deposed monarchs one can see at seedy summer resorts along the Adriatic. Close up, she looked softer, middle-class, and wholly alarming. Often as Christopher sat across from Miss Melbourne, trying to eat his lunch and at the same time answer her unexpected questions, he would recall a portrait he had seen of a Renaissance merchant's shrewd, hardy wife. It had something to do with Miss Melbourne's plump shoulders and small pink nose, with her habit of fingering the lockets and laces she wore as though drawing the artist's attention to essentials.'

"Miss Pugh had spent most of her life abroad, which was not unusual for rich spinsters of her generation. She seldom mentioned her father, a common fortune hunter, soon shed by her mother—tactful hostess, careful parent, trusted friend to artists and writers. The ash tree whose shade contributed no little to the primeval twilight of the dining room had grown from a sapling presented by Edith Wharton. As a girl, Miss Pugh had been allowed to peer round the door and watch her renowned compatriot eating sole meunière. She had not been presented to Mrs. Wharton, who was divorced.

"What constituted the difference between Mrs. Pugh, also divorced, and the novelist? It is likely that Miss Pugh never asked herself this question. Most of her interesting anecdotes drifted off in this way, into the haze of ancient social mystery.

"The house that was to be Victor Prism's refuge for a summer had been built in the eighteen-fifties, in a quiet street straggling downhill from the Trocadéro. Miss Pugh had inherited, along with the house, a legend that Balzac wrote *Cousine Bette* in the upstairs sitting room, though the prolific author had been buried a good three years before the foundation was dug. *Madame mère* probably bought the house in the eighteen-eighties. Soon after that, the character of the street changed. A considerable amount of low-value property changed hands. Most of the small houses were destroyed or became surrounded by seven-story apartment buildings made of stone, sturdily Third Republic in style. The house we are speaking of was now actually at the heart of a block, connected to the world by a narrow carriage drive, the latter a subject of perennial litigation. Tenants of the apartments could look down upon a low red-brick dwelling with a slate roof, an ash tree that managed to flourish without sunlight, dense thickets of indeterminate urban shrubbery, a bronze Italian birdbath, and a Cupid on tiptoe. The path from gate to door was always wet underfoot, like the floor of a forest.

"Inside, the rooms were low and dim, the floors warped and uneven. Coal fires burned to no great effect except further to darken the walls. Half the rooms by the nineteen-forties were shut off. Miss Pugh was no stingier than any other rich woman, nor had there as yet been an appreciable decline in her income. She was taking it for granted there would soon be another war, followed this time by the definitive revolution. Her daydreams were populated by Bolsheviks, swarming up the Trocadéro hill, waving eviction notices. Why create more comfort than one could bear to lose?

" 'To enjoy it, even for a minute' would have been the answer of a Victor Prism, or, for that matter, of any other of the gifted drifters for whom Paris had become a catchall, and to whom Miss Pugh offered conversation and asylum. Some were political refugees of the first postwar wave, regarded everywhere with immense suspicion. It was thought they should go back to wherever they'd come from and help build just, Spartan societies. Not so Miss Pugh, who thought they should sit down in one of the upstairs rooms and write about their mothers. Some were young men on the run from the legend of a heroic father, whose jaunty wartime face, smiling from a mantelshelf, was enough to launch any son into a life of firm and steady goldbricking. Some, like Prism, were trying to climb on the right American spring-board for a flying start.

" 'What is your ideal?' Miss Pugh liked to ask. 'At your age, you can't live without one.'

"Thirty, forty years ago, 'ideal' opened the way to tumble-down houses like Miss Pugh's that were really fairy castles. The moat was flooded with American generosity and American contrition. Probably no moat in history was ever so easy to bridge. (Any young European thinking of making that crossing today should be warned that the contrition silted up in the early nineteen-seventies, after which the castle was abandoned.) Miss Pugh did not expect gratitude for material favors, and would have considered it a base emotion. But she had no qualms about showing a stern face to any protégé who revealed himself to be untalented, bereft of an ideal in working order, mentally idle, or coarsely materialistic. This our poor Victor Prism was to learn before the summer was out. Miss Pugh belonged to a small Christian congregation that took its substance from Buddhism. She treated most living creatures equally and made little distinction between man and worm.

"How did Prism turn into a protégé? Easily; he rang a doorbell. Rosalia answered to a young man who was carrying a manila envelope, manuscript-sized, and a letter. She reached for the letter of introduction but did not let Prism in, even though large drops of rain had started to fall.

"Miss Pugh, upstairs in the Balzac sitting room, addressed, from the window, a troubled-looking patch of sky. 'Hasn't this been going on long enough?' Rosalia heard her say. 'Why don't you do something?'

"The answer to Miss Pugh's cosmic despair, or impertinence, was Victor Prism. She had been acknowledged by the universe before now, but perhaps never so quickly. She sat down with her back to the window, read the letter Rosalia gave her, folded it, thought it over, and said, 'All right. Bring him up.'

"Prism came into her presence with a step that lost its assurance as he drew near. He asked permission to sit down. Having obtained a nod, he placed his manila envelope on a low table, where Miss Pugh could reach it easily, and repeated everything she had just read in the letter: He was promising but poor. He had been staying with Mrs. Hartley-Greene on Avenue Gabriel. Mrs. Hartley-Greene had been indescribably helpful and kind. However, she was interested in painters, not in writers—particularly writers of prose.

"Miss Pugh said, 'Then you aren't that poet.'

" 'No, no,' said Prism. 'I am not that...that.'

"He was puzzled by the house, believing that it had deliberately been built at the heart of a hollow square, perhaps by a demented architect, for nonsensical people. Rain poured down on the ash tree and naked Cupid. In a flat across the way a kitchen light went on. Miss Pugh pressed the switch of a green-shaded lamp and considered Prism. He turned his head slightly and observed an oil painting of the martyrdom of St. Sebastian. He thought of mile upon mile of museum portraits—young men, young saints pierced with arrows, with nothing to protect them from the staring of women but a coat of varnish.

"The passage of the envelope from his hands to Miss Pugh's was crucial to his adventure. He wondered if he should speak. At the same time, he hated to let the envelope go. It held his entire capital—two chapters of a novel. He did not know if he would ever write anything better, or even if he could write anything else at all.

"Miss Pugh settled the matter by picking it up. 'It's for me to read, isn't it? I'll do so at once. Perhaps you could come back after dinner tonight.'

"*During* dinner would have suited Prism better: Mrs. Hartley-Greene was under the impression he had already moved out and would not be back except to pick up some luggage. *Goldfinches* gives a vivid account of his retreat: 'Christopher seemed to leave a trail of sawdust. There were arrow wounds everywhere. He did not know what other people thought and felt about anything, but he could sense to a fine degree how they thought and felt about him. He lived on the feelings he aroused, sought acquaintances among those in whom these feelings were not actively hostile, and did not know of any other way to be.'

"Eighty pages were in the envelope, thirty of them blank. Miss Pugh was not forced to spend every minute between tea and dinner reading, though she would have done so gladly. She read anything recommended to her, proceeding slowly, pausing often to wonder if the author was sure of his facts. She had a great fear of being hoodwinked, for she knew by now that in art deception is the rule.

"What Prism had described was an elderly duchess, a loyal old manservant named Norbert, a wounded pigeon, and a nation at war. His fifty completed pages were divided into two chapters.

"Chapter 1: In a city under siege, a duchess wonders how to save the priceless eighteenth-century china presented to her family by the Empress. Whatever food Norbert manages to forage she feeds to her cats. She and Norbert adopt and discard schemes for saving the china. They think about this and discuss it all day long.

"Chapter 2: A pigeon flutters in the window. A cat jumps at it, breaking its wing. The duchess and Norbert hear gunfire moving closer. They discuss a plan for saving the pigeon.

"That was as far as it went. Either Prism did not know what came next or did not want to say. It seemed to Miss Pugh that a good deal had been left in the air. The first thing she asked when he came back that night was if the china was really worth saving.

If it was priceless, as he claimed, then Norbert ought to pack it into cases lined with heavy silver paper. The cases could then be buried in the garden, if the ground was soft. That would depend on the season, which Prism had not described.

"She had begun a process that Prism had not foreseen and that was the most flattering success he might have imagined. Everything in the story was *hers*, from the duchess to the pigeon.

"Next, she gave her attention to the duchess's apartments, which seemed to be in the wing of a palace. Prism had not mentioned the style of architecture of the palace, or its condition. Most palaces nowadays were museums. Miss Pugh advised Prism to give the duchess an address more realistic and to eliminate from her life the threat of war.

"Then, at last, she said the only thing that mattered: she was ready to offer Prism the opportunity for creative endeavor Mrs. Hartley-Greene had been obliged to refuse because of her predilection for painters. Prism could return in the morning, by which time Rosalia would have his room ready. In the meantime, Miss Pugh would comb through the manuscript again.

"In *Goldfinches*, Prism skims over the next few hours. We have only the testimony of Rosalia, which is that he turned up in the morning looking as if he had spent the night curled up in a doorway.

"Miss Pugh was eating her breakfast in the sitting room with the green-shaded lamp and the portrait of St. Sebastian. Through a half-open door Prism caught a glimpse of her large, canopied bed. There was an extra place laid at the table.

" 'I was expecting my brother,' said Miss Pugh. 'But he has been delayed.'

"Instead of breakfast, Pugh was to have the manila envelope. In his account of the scene, Prism makes a curious mistake: 'The morning sun, kept from Christopher by the angle of the yellow awning, slid into view and hit him square in the face. His eyes watered, and as if a film of illusion had been removed. . .' and so on. There was no awning, no sun; the house was down a well.

"Miss Pugh asked Prism what he thought of Picasso. He understood the question as a test. Her rooms gave no clue to her own opinion; there were no Picassos in sight, but that was not to say there never could be. He drew a square in his mind, as a way of steadying his thoughts, and put Picasso in it.

"All at once, in a rush of blinding anger, he knew what he believed. His first words were inaudible, but as he regained hold on his feelings the sense of his wild protest became clear: 'All that money. All that *money*. Does he enjoy it? They say he lives in the kitchen, like a squatter. As if the house did not belong to him. He could travel. He could own things. He could have twenty-two servants. He does not deserve to have a fortune, because he doesn't know how to use one.'

"His hostess plucked at her table napkin. She was accustomed to hearing poor young men say what they could do with money. She had heard the hunger in the voice, the incoherence and the passion. She had often aroused this longing, putting out the bait and withdrawing it, which was the only form of wickedness she knew. She seemed to be reflecting on what Prism had just said. There was no denying it was original. Who ever had seen Picasso at an auction of rare furniture? At the races, straining after one of his own horses? Photographed at a gala evening in Monte Carlo? Boarding a yacht for a cruise in Greek waters?

"'What do you think?' said Prism boldly.

"'He is the most attractive man in the world. My brother would look good, too, if he could stop drinking and pull himself together. What's your opinion of his goats?' Prism shook his head. 'The sculpture. You can see Picasso doesn't care for animals. Those goats are half starved. I suppose you'll be wanting to get to work.'

"Prism in a very short time came to the conclusion he had climbed on the wrong springboard. He saw that the anxiety and frustration of patronage, the backer's terror of being duped, of having been taken in, was second only to the protégé's fear of being despoiled, stripped, robbed, and left bankrupt by the side of the road. Miss Pugh did not loosen her grip on his two chapters, and even Prism's decision that he wanted to have nothing more to do with them did not lessen the tension.

"He would not claim those two chapters today. If they followed him in the street, he would probably threaten them with an umbrella. And yet the story is his; it is *his* duchess, *his* rustic bandstand. It was also Miss Pugh's. 'Have you moved that poor woman out of that filthy old palace yet?' she would ask Prism at lunch. 'Have you found out any more about the china?' When the leaves of Mrs. Wharton's ash tree began to droop and turn yellow, patroness and protégé were at a stalemate that could be ended only by sincere admission of defeat. Miss Pugh was in her own house; Prism had to play the loser. One day he sat down at the Louis XVI period table in his room and considered the blank pages still in the manila envelope. He wondered if the time had not come to return to England, try for a good degree, and then teach.

" 'I can always branch out from there,' he said to himself. (How easy it must have sounded.)

"He saw in his mind the museum rooms full of portraits of St. Sebastian, with nothing for protection but a thin coat of varnish. There were two opinions about the conservation of art. One claimed it was a mistake to scour paintings in order to lay bare the original color. The other believed it was essential to do so, even if the artist had made allowances for the mellowing and darkening effect of the glaze, and even if the colors revealed turned out to be harsher than the artist had intended. Prism drew a blank sheet toward him and began to write, 'Are we to take it for granted that the artist thinks he knows what he is doing?' At that moment, Prism the critic was born.

"Miss Pugh was sorry when she heard he wanted to give up the duchess, but it was not her policy to engage the Muses in battle. Prism presented her with the manuscript; she gave him the crêpe-soled shoes. She was never heard to speak of him slightingly, and she read with generous pleasure all the newspaper cuttings concerning himself that he sent her over the years. Whenever he came to Paris Miss Pugh would ask him to tea and rejoiced in the rich texture of his career, which he unfolded by the hour, without tiring speaker or audience. Prism made Miss Pugh the subject of countless comic anecdotes and the central female character of *Goldfinches*. He was always evenhanded."

A nother Easter went by before Grippes received an acknowledgment—a modest check in lieu of the promised fee, and an apology: His memoir had been mailed to Victor Prism to be checked for accuracy, and Prism had still not replied. During the year sweeping changes had been made. The *Angliciste* had published a paper on the Common Market as seen through English fiction. It was felt to contain a political bias, and the Ministry had withdrawn support. The publisher had no choice but to replace him as editor by the only responsible person who seemed to be free at the time, a famous *Irlandiste* on leave from a university in Belgium. The *Irlandiste* restored the project to its original three volumes, threw out the English section as irrelevant, and added a division with potted biographies of eight hundred Irish poets favorable to France and the Common Market.

Grippes has heard that it is to be published in 2010, at the very latest. He knows that in the meantime they are bound to call on him again—more and more as time goes on. He is the only person still alive with any sort of memory.

GRIPPES AND POCHE

At an early hour for the French man of letters Henri Grippes—it was a quarter to nine, on an April morning—he sat in a windowless, brown-painted cubicle, facing a slight, mop-headed young man with horn-rimmed glasses and dimples. The man wore a dark tie with a narrow knot and a buttoned-up blazer. His signature was "O. Poche"; his title, on the grubby, pulpy summons Grippes had read, sweating, was "Controller." He must be freshly out of his civil-service training school, Grippes guessed. Even his aspect, of a priest hearing a confession a few yards from the guillotine, seemed newly acquired. Before him lay open a dun-colored folder with not much in it—a letter from Grippes, full of delaying tactics, and copies of his correspondence with a bank in California. It was not true that American banks protected a depositor's secrets; anyway, this one hadn't. Another reason Grippes thought O. Poche must be recent was the way he kept blushing. He was not nearly as pale or as case-hardened as Grippes.

At this time, President de Gaulle had been in power five years, two of which Grippes had spent in blithe writer-in-residenceship in California. Returning to Paris, he had left a bank account behind. It was forbidden, under the Fifth Republic, for a French citizen to have a foreign account. The government might not have cared so much about drachmas or zlotys, but dollars were supposed to be scraped in, converted to francs at bottom rate, and, of course, counted as personal income. Grippes' unwise and furtive moves with trifling sums, his somewhat paranoid disagreements with California over exchange, had finally caught the eye of the Bank of France, as a glistening minnow might attract a dozing whale. The whale swallowed Grippes, found him too small to matter, and spat him out, straight into the path of a water ox called Public Treasury, Direct Taxation, Personal Income. That was Poche.

What Poche had to discuss—a translation of Grippes' novel, the one about the French teacher at the American university and his doomed love affair with his student, Karen-Sue—seemed to embarrass him. Observing Poche with some curiosity, Grippes saw, unreeling, scenes from the younger man's inhibited boyhood. He sensed, then discerned, the Catholic boarding school in bleakest Brittany: the unheated forty-bed dormitory, a nightly torment of unchaste dreams with astonishing partners, a daytime terror of real Hell with real fire.

"Human waywardness is hardly new," said Grippes, feeling more secure now that he had tested Poche and found him provincial. "It no longer shocks anyone."

It was not the moral content of the book he wished to talk over, said Poche, flaming. In any case, he was not qualified to do so: he had flubbed Philosophy and never taken Modern French Thought. (He must be new, Grippes decided. He was babbling.) Frankly, even though he had the figures in front of him, Poche found it hard to believe the American translation had earned its author so little. There must be another considerable sum, placed in some other bank. Perhaps M. Grippes could try to remember.

The figures were true. The translation had done poorly. Failure played to Grippes' advantage, reducing the hint of

deliberate tax evasion to a simple oversight. Still, it hurt to have
things put so plainly. He felt bound to tell Poche that American
readers were no longer interested in the teacher-student imbro-
glio, though there had been some slight curiosity as to what a
foreigner might wring out of the old sponge.

Poche gazed at Grippes. His eyes seemed to Grippes as
helpless and eager as those of a gun dog waiting for a command
in the right language. Encouraged, Grippes said more: in writing
his novel, he had overlooked the essential development—the
erring professor was supposed to come home at the end. He
could be half dead, limping, on crutches, toothless, jobless, broke,
impotent—it didn't matter. He had to be judged and shriven. As
further mortification, his wife during his foolish affair would have
gone on to be a world-class cellist, under her maiden name.
"Wife" had not entered Grippes' cast of characters, probably
because, like Poche, he did not have one. (He had noticed Poche
did not wear a wedding ring.) Grippes had just left his professor
driving off to an airport in blessed weather, whistling a jaunty air.

Poche shook his head. Obviously, it was not the language he
was after. He began to write on a clean page of the file, taking no
more notice of Grippes.

What a mistake it had been, Grippes reflected, still feeling
pain beneath the scar, to have repeated the male teacher–female
student pattern. He should have turned it around, identified
himself with a brilliant and cynical woman teacher. Unfortunately, unlike Flaubert (his academic stalking-horse), he could
not put himself in a woman's place, probably because he thought
it an absolutely terrible place to be. The novel had not done well
in France, either. (Poche had still to get round to that.) The
critics had found Karen-Sue's sociological context obscure. She
seemed at a remove from events of her time, unaware of
improved literacy figures in North Korea, never once mentioned, or that since the advent of Gaullism it cost twenty-five
centimes to mail a letter. The Pill was still unheard of in much of
Europe; readers could not understand what it was Karen-Sue

kept forgetting to take, or why Grippes had devoted a contemplative no-action chapter to the abstract essence of risk. The professor had not given Karen-Sue the cultural and political enlightenment one might expect from the graduate of a pre-eminent Paris school. It was a banal story, really, about a pair of complacently bourgeois lovers. The real victim was Grippes, seduced and abandoned by the American middle class.

It was Grippes' first outstanding debacle and, for that reason, the only one of his works he ever reread. He could still hear Karen-Sue—the true, the original—making of every avowal a poignant question: "I'm Cairn-Sioux? I know you're busy? It's just that I don't understand what you said about Flaubert and his own niece?" He recalled her with tolerance—the same tolerance that had probably weakened the book.

Grippes was wise enough to realize that the California-bank affair had been an act of folly, a con man's aberration. He had thought he would get away with it, knowing all the while he could not. There existed a deeper treasure for Poche to uncover, well below Public Treasury sights. Computers had not yet come into government use; even typewriters were rare—Poche had summoned Grippes in a cramped, almost secretive hand. It took time to strike an error, still longer to write a letter about it. In his youth, Grippes had received from an American patroness of the arts three rent-bearing apartments in Paris, which he still owned. (The patroness had been the last of a generous species, Grippes one of the last young men to benefit from her kind.) He collected the rents by devious and untraceable means, stowing the cash obtained in safe deposit. His visible way of life was stoic and plain; not even the most vigilant Controller could fault his underfurnished apartment in Montparnasse, shared with some cats he had already tried to claim as dependents. He showed none of the signs of prosperity Public Treasury seemed to like, such as membership in a golf club.

After a few minutes of speculative anguish in the airless cubicle, Grippes saw that Poche had no inkling whatever about the flats. He was chasing something different—the inexistent royalties from the Karen-Sue novel. By a sort of divine even-handedness, Grippes was going to have to pay for imaginary earnings. He put the safe deposit out of his mind, so that it would not show on his face, and said, "What will be left for me, when you've finished adding and subtracting?"

To his surprise, Poche replied in a bold tone, pitched for reciting quotations: "'What is left? What is left? Only what remains at low tide, when small islands are revealed, emerging...'" He stopped quoting and flushed. Obviously, he had committed the worst sort of blunder, had been intimate, had let his own personality show. He had crossed over to his opponent's ground.

"It sounds familiar," said Grippes, enticing him further. "Although, to tell the truth, I don't remember writing it."

"It is a translation," said Poche. "The Anglo-Saxon British author, Victor Prism." He pronounced it "Prissom."

"You've read Prism?" said Grippes, pronouncing correctly the name of an old acquaintance.

"I had to. Prissom was on the preparatory program. Anglo-Saxon Commercial English."

"They stuffed you with foreign writers?" said Grippes. "With so many of us having to go to foreign lands for a living?"

That was perilous: he had just challenged Poche's training, the very foundation of his right to sit there reading Grippes' private mail. But he had suddenly recalled his dismay when as a young man he had looked at a shelf in his room and realized he had to compete with the dead—Proust, Flaubert, Balzac, Stendhal, and on into the dark. The rivalry was infinite, a Milky Way of dead stars still daring to shine. He had invented a law, a moratorium on publication that would eliminate the dead, leaving the skies clear for the living. (All the living? Grippes still couldn't decide.) Foreign writers would be deported to a remote solar system, where they could circle one another.

For Prism, there was no system sufficiently remote. Not so

long ago, interviewed in *The Listener*, Prism had dragged in Grippes, saying that he used to cross the Channel to consult a seer in Half Moon Street, hurrying home to set down the prose revealed from a spirit universe. "Sometimes I actually envied him," Prism was quoted as saying. He sounded as though Grippes were dead. "I used to wish ghost voices would speak to me, too," suggesting ribbons of pure Prism running like ticker tape round the equator of a crystal ball. "Unfortunately, I had to depend on my own creative intelligence, modest though I am sure it was."

Poche did not know about this recent libel in Anglo-Saxon Commercial English. He had been trying to be nice. Grippes made a try of his own, jocular: "I only meant, you could have been reading *me*." The trouble was that he meant it, ferociously.

Poche must have heard the repressed shout. He shut the file and said, "This dossier is too complex for my level. I shall have to send it up to the Inspector." Grippes made a vow that he would never let natural pique get the better of him again.

" W hat will be left for me?" Grippes asked the Inspector. "When you have finished adding and subtracting?"

Mme. de Pelle did not bother to look up. She said, "Somebody should have taken this file in hand a long time ago. Let us start at the beginning. How long, in all, were you out of the country?"

When Poche said "send up," he'd meant it literally. Grippes looked out on a church where Delacroix had worked and the slow summer rain. At the far end of the square, a few dark shops displayed joyfully trashy religious goods, like the cross set with tiny seashells Mme. de Pelle wore round her neck. Grippes had been raised in an anticlerical household, in a small town where opposing factions were grouped behind the schoolmaster— Grippes' father—and the parish priest. Women, lapsed agnostics, sometimes crossed enemy lines and started going to church. One glimpsed them, all in gray, creeping along a gray-walled street.

"You are free to lodge a protest against the fine," said Mme. de Pelle. "But if you lose the contestation, your fine will be tripled. That is the law."

Grippes decided to transform Mme. de Pelle into the manager of a brothel catering to the Foreign Legion, slovenly in her habits and addicted to chloroform, but he found the idea unpromising. In due course he paid a monstrous penalty, which he did not contest, for fear of drawing attention to the apartments. (It was still believed that he had stashed away millions from the Karen-Sue book, probably in Switzerland.) A summons addressed in O. Poche's shrunken hand, the following spring, showed Grippes he had been tossed back downstairs. After that he forgot about Mme. de Pelle, except now and then.

It was at about this time that a series of novels offered themselves to Grippes—shadowy outlines behind a frosted-glass pane. He knew he must not let them crowd in all together, or keep them waiting too long. His foot against the door, he admitted, one by one, a number of shadows that turned into young men, each bringing his own name and address, his native region of France portrayed on color postcards, and an index of information about his tastes in clothes, love, food, and philosophers, his bent of character, his tics of speech, his attitudes toward God and money, his political bias, and the intimation of a crisis about to explode underfoot. "Antoine" provided a Jesuit confessor, a homosexual affinity, and loss of faith. Spiritual shilly-shallying tends to run long; Antoine's covered more than six hundred pages, making it the thickest work in the Grippes canon. Then came "Thomas," with his Spartan mother on a Provençal fruit farm, rejected in favor of a civil-service career. "Bertrand" followed, adrift in frivolous Paris, tempted by neo-Fascism in the form of a woman wearing a bedjacket trimmed with marabou. "René" cycled round France, reading Chateaubriand when he stopped to rest. One morning he set fire to the barn he had been sleeping in, leaving his books to burn. This was the shortest of the novels, and the most popular with the young. One critic scolded Grippes for using crude symbolism. Another begged him to stop hiding behind "Antoine" and "René" and to take the metaphysical risk of revealing "Henri." But Grippes had tried that once with Karen-Sue, then with a roman à clef mercifully destroyed in the confusion of May, 1968. He took these contretemps for a sign that he was to leave the subjective Grippes alone. The fact that each novel appeared even to Grippes to be a slice of French writing about life as it had been carved up and served a generation before made it seem quietly insurrectional. Nobody was doing this now; no one but Grippes. Grippes, for a time uneasy, decided to go on letting the shadows in.

The announcement of a new publication would bring a summons from Poche. When Poche leaned over the file, now, Grippes saw amid the mop of curls a coin-sized tonsure. His diffident, steely questions tried to elicit from Grippes how many copies were likely to be sold and where Grippes had already put the money. Grippes would give him a copy of the book, inscribed. Poche would turn back the cover and glance at the signature, probably to make certain Grippes had not written something compromising and friendly. He kept the novels in a metal locker, fastened together with government-issue webbing tape and a military-looking buckle. It troubled Grippes to think of his work all in a bundle, in the dark. He thought of old-fashioned milestones, half hidden by weeds, along disused roads. The volumes marked time for Poche, too. He was still a Controller. Perhaps he had to wait for the woman upstairs to retire, so he could take over her title and office. The cubicle needed paint. There was a hole in the brown linoleum, just inside the door. Poche now wore a wedding ring. Grippes wondered if he should congratulate him, but decided to let Poche mention the matter first. He tried to imagine Mme. Poche.

Grippes could swear that in his string of novels nothing had been chipped out of his own past. Antoine, Thomas, Bertrand, and René (and, by now, Clément, Didier, Laurent, Hugues, and Yves) had arrived as strangers, almost like historical figures. At the same time, it seemed to Grippes that their wavering, ruffled reflection should deliver something he alone might recognize. What did he see, bending over the pond of his achievement? He saw a character close-mouthed, cautious, unimaginative, ill at ease, obsessed with particulars. Worse, he was closed against progress, afraid of reform, shut into a literary, reactionary France. How could this be? Grippes had always and sincerely voted left. He had proved he could be reckless, open-minded, indulgent. He was like a father gazing round the breakfast table and suddenly realizing that none of the children are his. His children, if he could call them that, did not even look like him. From Antoine to Yves, his reflected character was small and slight, with a mop of curly hair, horn-rimmed glasses, and dimples.

Grippes believed in the importance of errors. No political system, no love affair, no native inclination, no life itself would be tolerable without a wide mesh for mistakes to slip through. It pleased him that Public Treasury had never caught up with the three apartments—not just for the sake of the cash piling up in safe deposit but for the black hole of error revealed. He and Poche had been together for some years—another blunder. Usually Controller and taxpayer were torn apart after a meeting or two, so that the revenue service would not start taking into consideration the client's aged indigent aunt, his bill for dental surgery, his alimony payments, his perennial mortgage. But possibly no one except Poche could be bothered with Grippes, always making some time-wasting claim for minute professional expenses, backed by a messy-looking certified receipt. Sometimes Grippes dared believe Poche admired him, that he hung on to the dossier out of devotion to his books. (This conceit was intensified when Poche began calling him "*Maître*.") Once, Grippes won some City of Paris award and was shown in *France-Soir* shaking hands with the mayor and simultaneously receiving a long, check-filled envelope. Immediately summoned by Poche, expecting a discreet compliment, Grippes found him interested

only in the caption under the photo, which made much of the
size of the check. Grippes later thought of sending a sneering
letter—"Thank you for your warm congratulations"—but he
decided in time it was wiser not to fool with Poche. Poche had
recently given him a thirty-three-per-cent personal exemption,
three per cent more than the outer limit for Grippes' category of
unsalaried earners—according to Poche, a group that included,
as well as authors, door-to-door salesmen and prostitutes.

The dun-colored Gaullist-era jacket on Grippes' file had worn
out long ago and been replaced, in 1969, by a cover in cool
banker's green. Green presently made way for a shiny black-and-
white marbled effect, reflecting the mood of opulence of the
early seventies. Called in for his annual springtime confession,
Grippes remarked about the folder: "Culture seems to have
taken a decisive turn."

Poche did not ask what culture. He continued bravely, "Food
for the cats, *Maître*. We *can't*."

"They depend on me," said Grippes. But they had already
settled the cats-as-dependents question once and for all. Poche
drooped over Grippes' smudged and unreadable figures. Grippes
tried to count the number of times he had examined the top of
Poche's head. He still knew nothing about Poche, except for the
wedding ring. Somewhere along the way, Poche had tied himself
to a need for retirement pay and rich exemptions of his own. In
the language of his generation, Poche was a fully structured
individual. His vocabulary was sparse and to the point, centered
on a single topic. His state training school, the machine that
ground out Pelles and Poches all sounding alike, was in Cler-
mont-Ferrand. Grippes was born in the same region. That might
have given them something else to talk about, except that
Grippes had never been back. Structured Poche probably
attended class reunions, was godfather to classmates' children,
jotted their birthdays in a leather-covered notebook he never
mislaid. Unstructured Grippes could not even remember his
own age.

Poche turned over a sheet of paper, read something Grippes could not see, and said, automatically, *"We can't."*

"Nothing is ever as it was," said Grippes, still going on about the marbled-effect folder. It was a remark that usually shut people up, leaving them nowhere to go but a change of subject. Besides, it was true. Nothing can be as it was. Poche and Grippes had just lost a terrifying number of brain cells. They were an instant closer to death. Death was of no interest to Poche. If he ever thought he might cease to exist, he would stop concentrating on other people's business and get down to reading Grippes while there was still time. Grippes wanted to ask, "Do you ever imagine your own funeral?," but it might have been taken as a threatening, gangsterish hint from taxpayer to Controller—worse, far worse, than an attempted bribe.

A folder of a pretty mottled-peach shade appeared. Poche's cubicle was painted soft beige, the torn linoleum repaired. Poche sat in a comfortable armchair resembling the wide leathery seats in smart furniture stores at the upper end of Boulevard Saint-Germain. Grippes had a new, straight metallic chair that shot him bolt upright and hurt his spine. It was the heyday of the Giscardian period, when it seemed more important to keep the buttons polished than to watch where the regiment was heading. Grippes and Poche had not advanced one inch toward each other. Except for the paint and the chairs and *"Maître,"* it could have been 1963. No matter how many works were added to the bundle in the locker, no matter how often Grippes had his picture taken, no matter how many Grippes paperbacks blossomed on airport bookstalls, Grippes to Poche remained a button.

The mottled-peach jacket began to darken and fray. Poche said to Grippes, "I asked you to come here, *Maître*, because I find we have overlooked something concerning your income." Grippes' heart gave a lurch. "The other day I came across an old ruling about royalties. How much of your income do you kick back?"

"Excuse me?"

"To publishers, to bookstores," said Poche. "How much?"

"Kick back?"

"What percentage?" said Poche. "Publishers. Printers."

"You mean," said Grippes, after a time, "how much do I pay editors to edit, publishers to publish, printers to print, and booksellers to sell?" He supposed that to Poche such a scheme might sound plausible. It would fit his long view over Grippes' untidy life. Grippes knew most of the literary gossip that went round about himself; the circle was so small that it had to come back. In most stories there was a virus of possibility, but he had never heard anything as absurd as this, or as base.

Poche opened the file, concealing the moldering cover, apparently waiting for Grippes to mention a figure. The nausea Grippes felt he put down to his having come here without breakfast. One does not insult a Controller. He had shouted silently at Poche, years before, and had been sent upstairs to do penance with Mme. de Pelle. It is not good to kick over a chair and stalk out. "I have never been so insulted!" might have no meaning from Grippes, keelhauled month after month in one lumpy review or another. As his works increased from bundle to heap, so they drew intellectual abuse. He welcomed partisan ill-treatment, as warming to him as popular praise. Don't forget me, Grippes silently prayed, standing at the periodicals table in La Hune, the Left Bank bookstore, looking for his own name in those quarterlies no one ever takes home. Don't praise me. Praise is weak stuff. Praise me after I'm dead.

But even the most sour and despairing and close-printed essays were starting to mutter acclaim. The shoreline of the eighties, barely in sight, was ready to welcome Grippes, who had re-established the male as hero, whose left-wing heartbeat could be heard, loyally thumping, behind the armor of his right-wing traditional prose. His re-established hero had curly hair, soft eyes, horn-rimmed glasses, dimples, and a fully structured life. He was pleasing to both sexes and to every type of reader, except for a few thick-ribbed louts. Grippes looked back at Poche, who did not know how closely they were bound. What if he were to say, "This is a preposterous insinuation, a blot on a noble profession and on my reputation in particular," only to have Poche answer, "Too bad, *Maître*—I was trying to help"? He said, as one good-natured fellow to another, "Well, what if I own up to this crime?"

"It's no crime," said Poche. "I simply add the amount to your professional expenses."

"To my rebate?" said Grippes. "To my exemption?"

"It depends on how much."

"A third of my income?" said Grippes, insanely. "Half?"

"A reasonable figure might be twelve and a half per cent."

All this for Grippes. Poche wanted nothing. Grippes considered with awe the only uncorruptible element in a porous society. No secret message had passed between them. He could not even invite Poche to lunch. He wondered if this arrangement had ever actually existed—if there could possibly be a good dodge that he, Grippes, had never heard of. He thought of contemporary authors for whose success there could be no other explanation: it had to be celestial playfulness or twelve and a half per cent. The structure, as Grippes was already calling it, might also just be Poche's innocent, indecent idea about writers.

Poche was reading the file again, though he must have known everything in it by heart. He was as absorbed, as contented, and somehow as pure as a child with a box of paints. At any moment he would raise his tender, bewildered eyes and murmur, "Four dozen typewriter ribbons in a third of the fiscal year, *Maître*? We *can't*."

Grippes tried to compose a face for Poche to encounter, a face above reproach. But writers considered above reproach always looked moody and haggard, about to scream. "Be careful," he was telling himself. "Don't let Poche think he's doing you a favor. These people set traps." Was Poche angling for something? Was this bait? "Attempting to bribe a public servant" the accusation was called. "Bribe" wasn't the word: it was "corruption" the law mentioned—"an attempt to corrupt." All Grippes had ever offered Poche was his books, formally inscribed, as though Poche were an anonymous reader standing in line in a bookstore where Grippes, wedged behind a shaky table, sat signing away. "Your name?" "Whose name?" "How do you spell your name?" "Oh, the book isn't for me. It's for a friend of mine." His look changed to one of severity and impatience, until he remembered that Poche had never asked him to sign anything. He had never concealed his purpose, to pluck from Grippes' plumage every bright feather he could find.

"Careful," Grippes repeated. "Careful. Remember what happened to Prism."

Victor Prism, keeping pale under a parasol on the beach at Torremolinos, had made the acquaintance of a fellow-Englishman—pleasant, not well educated but eager to learn, blistered shoulders, shirt draped over his head, pages of the *Sunday Express* round his red thighs. Prism lent him something to read—his sunburn was keeping him awake. It was a creative essay on three émigré authors of the nineteen-thirties, in a review so obscure and ill-paying that Prism had not bothered to include the fee on his income-tax return. (Prism had got it wrong, of course, having Thomas Mann—whose plain name Prism could not spell—go to East Germany and with his wife start a theatre that presented his own plays, sending Stefan Zweig to be photographed with movie stars in California, and putting Bertolt Brecht to die a bitter man in self-imposed exile in Brazil. As it turned out, none of Prism's readers knew the difference. Chided by Grippes, Prism had been defensive, cold, said that no letters had come in. "One, surely?" said Grippes. "Yes, I thought that must be you," Prism said.)

Prism might have got off with the whole thing if his new friend had not fallen sound asleep after the first lines. Waking, refreshed, he had said to himself, "I must find out what they get paid for this stuff," a natural reflex—he was of the Inland Revenue. He'd found no trace, no record; for Inland Revenue purposes "Death and Exile" did not exist. The subsequent fine was so heavy and Prism's disgrace so acute that he fled England to spend a few days with Grippes and the cats in Montparnasse. He sat on a kitchen chair while Grippes, nose and mouth protected by a checked scarf, sprayed terror to cockroaches. Prism, weeping in the fumes and wiping his eyes, said, "I'm through with Queen and Country"—something like that—"and I'm taking out French citizenship tomorrow."

"You would have to marry a Frenchwoman and have at least five male children," said Grippes, through the scarf. He was feeling the patriotic hatred of a driver on a crowded road seeing foreign license plates in the way.

"Oh, well, then," said Prism, as if to say, "I won't bother."

"Oh, well, then," said Grippes, softly, not quite to Poche. Poche added one last thing to the file and closed it, as if something definite had taken place. He clasped his hands and placed them on the dossier; it seemed shut for all time now, like a grave. He said, "*Maître*, one never stays long in the same fiscal theatre. I have been in this one for an unusual length of time. We may not meet again. I want you to know I have enjoyed our conversations."

"So have I," said Grippes, with caution.

"Much of your autobiographical creation could apply to other lives of our time, believe me."

"So you have read them," said Grippes, an eye on the locker.

"I read those I bought," said Poche.

"But they are the same books."

"No. The books I bought belong to me. The others were gifts. I would never open a gift. I have no right to." His voice rose, and he spoke more slowly. "In one of them, when What's-His-Name struggles to prepare his civil-service tests, '. . .the desire for individual glory seemed so inapposite, suddenly, in a nature given to renunciation.' "

"I suppose it *is* a remarkable observation," said Grippes. "I was not referring to myself." He had no idea what that could be from, and he was certain he had not written it.

Poche did not send for Grippes again. Grippes became a commonplace taxpayer, filling out his forms without help. The frosted-glass door was reverting to dull white; there were fewer shadows for Grippes to let in. A fashion for having well-behaved Nazi officers shore up Western culture gave Grippes a chance to turn Poche into a tubercular poet, trapped in Paris by poverty and the Occupation. Grippes threw out the first draft, in which Poche joined a Christian-minded Resistance network and performed a few simple miracles, unaware of his own powers. He had the instinctive feeling that a new generation would not know what he was talking about. Instead, he placed Poche, sniffling and wheezing, in a squalid hotel room, cough pastilles spilled on the table, a stained blanket pinned round his shoulders. Up the fetid staircase came a handsome colonel, a Curt Jurgens type, smelling of shaving lotion, bent on saving liberal values, bringing Poche butter, cognac, and a thousand sheets of writing paper.

After that, Grippes no longer felt sure where to go. His earlier books, government tape and buckle binding them into an œuvre, had accompanied Poche to his new fiscal theatre. Perhaps, finding his career blocked by the woman upstairs, he had asked for early retirement. Poche was in a gangster-ridden Mediterranean city, occupying a shoddy boom-period apartment he'd spent twenty years paying for. He was working at black-market jobs, tax adviser to the local mayor, a small innocent cog in the regional Mafia. After lunch, Poche would sit on one of those southern balconies that hold just a deck chair, rereading in chronological order all Grippes' books. In the late afternoon, blinds drawn, Poche totted up Mafia accounts by a chink of light. Grippes was here, in Montparnasse, facing a flat-white glass door.

He continued to hand himself a forty-five-and-a-half-per-cent personal exemption—the astonishing thirty-three plus the unheard-of twelve and a half. No one seemed to mind. No shabby envelope holding an order for execution came in the mail. Sometimes in Grippes' mind a flicker of common sense flamed like revealed truth: the exemption was an error. Public Treasury was now tiptoeing toward computers. The computer brain was bound to wince at Grippes and stop functioning until the Grippes exemption was settled. Grippes rehearsed: "I was seriously misinformed."

He had to go farther and farther abroad to find offal for the cats. One tripe dealer had been turned into a driving school, another sold second-hand clothes. Returning on a winter evening after a long walk, carrying a parcel of sheep's lung wrapped in newspaper, he crossed Boulevard du Montparnasse just as the lights went on—the urban moonrise. The street was a dream street, faces flat white in the winter mist. It seemed to Grippes that he had crossed over to the nineteen-eighties, had only just noticed the new decade. In a recess between two glassed-in sidewalk cafés, four plainclothes cops were beating up a pair of pickpockets. Nobody had to explain the scene to Grippes; he knew what it was about. One prisoner already wore handcuffs. Customers on the far side of the glass gave no more than a glance. When they had got handcuffs on the second man, the cops pushed the two into the entrance of Grippes' apartment building to wait for the police van. Grippes shuffled into a café. He put his parcel of lights on the zinc-topped bar and started to read an article on the wrapping. Someone unknown to him, a new name, pursued an old grievance: Why don't they write about real life anymore?

Because to depict life is to attract its ill-fortune, Grippes replied.

He stood sipping coffee, staring at nothing. Four gun-bearing young men in jeans and leather jackets were not final authority; final authority was something written, the printed word, even when the word was mistaken. The simplest final authority in Grippes' life had been O. Poche and a book of rules. What must have happened was this: Poche, wishing to do honor to a category that included writers, prostitutes, and door-to-door salesmen, had read and misunderstood a note about royalties. It had been in italics, at the foot of the page. He had transformed his mistake into a regulation and had never looked at the page again.

Grippes in imagination climbed three flights of dirty wooden stairs to Mme. de Pelle's office. He observed the seashell crucifix and a brooch he had not noticed the first time, a silver fawn curled up as nature had never planned—a boneless fawn. Squinting, Mme. de Pelle peered at the old dun-colored Gaullist-era file. She put her hand over a page, as though Grippes were trying to read upside down. "It has all got to be paid back," she said.

"I was seriously misinformed," Grippes intended to answer, willing to see Poche disgraced, ruined, jailed. "I followed instructions. I am innocent."

But Poche had vanished, leaving Grippes with a lunatic exemption, three black-market income-bearing apartments he had recently, unsuccessfully, tried to sell, and a heavy reputation for male-oriented, left-feeling, right-thinking books. This reputation Grippes thought he could no longer sustain. A Socialist government was at last in place (hence his hurry about unloading the flats and his difficulty in finding takers). He wondered about the new file cover. Pink? Too fragile—look what had happened with the mottled peach. Strong denim blue, the shade standing for *giovinezza* and workers' overalls? It was no time for a joke, not even a private one. No one could guess what would be wanted, now, in the way of literary entertainment. The fitfulness of voters is such that, having got the government they wanted, they were now reading nothing but the right-wing press. Perhaps a steady right-wing heartbeat ought to set the cadence for a left-

wing outlook, with a complex, bravely conservative heroine
contained within the slippery but unyielding walls of left-wing
style. He would have to come to terms with the rightist way of
considering female characters. There seemed to be two methods,
neither of which suited Grippes' temperament: treat her disgust-
ingly, then cry all over the page, or admire and respect her—she
is the equal at least of a horse. The only woman his imagination
offered, with some insistence, was no use to him. She moved
quietly on a winter evening to Saint-Nicolas-du-Chardonnet, the
rebel church at the lower end of Boulevard Saint-Germain,
where services were still conducted in Latin. She wore a hat
ornamented with an ivory arrow, and a plain gray coat, tubular in
shape, with a narrow fur collar. Kid gloves were tucked under the
handle of her sturdy leather purse. She had never heard of video
games, push-button telephones, dishwashers, frozen filleted sole,
computer horoscopes. She entered the church and knelt down
and brought out her rosary, oval pearls strung on thin gold.
Nobody saw rosaries anymore. They were not even in the
windows of their traditional venues, across the square from the
tax bureau. Believers went in for different articles now: cherub
candles, quick prayers on plastic cards. Her iron meekness
resisted change. She prayed constantly into the past. Grippes
knew that one's view of the past is just as misleading as speculation about the future. It was one of the few beliefs he would have
gone to the stake for. She was praying to a mist, to mist-shrouded
figures she persisted in seeing clear.

He could see the woman, but he could not approach her.
Perhaps he could get away with dealing with her from a distance.
All that was really needed for a sturdy right-wing novel was its
pessimistic rhythm: and then, and then, and then, and death.
Grippes had that rhythm. It was in his footsteps, coming up the
stairs after the departure of the police van, turning the key in his
triple-bolted front door. And then, and then, the cats padding and
mewing, not giving Grippes time to take off his coat as they made
for their empty dishes on the kitchen floor. Behind the gas stove,

a beleaguered garrison of cockroaches got ready for the evening sortie. Grippes would be waiting, his face half veiled with a checked scarf.

In Saint-Nicolas-du-Chardonnet the woman shut her missal, got up off her knees, scorning to brush her coat; she went out to the street, proud of the dust marks, letting the world know she still prayed the old way. She escaped him. He had no idea what she had on, besides the hat and coat. Nobody else wore a hat with an ivory arrow or a tubular coat or a scarf that looked like a weasel biting its tail. He could not see what happened when she took the hat and coat off, what her hair was like, if she hung the coat in a hall closet that also contained umbrellas, a carpet sweeper, and a pile of old magazines, if she put the hat in a round box on a shelf. She moved off in a gray blur. There was a streaming window between them Grippes could not wipe clean. Probably she entered a dark dining room—fake Henri IV buffet, bottles of pills next to the oil and vinegar cruets, lace tablecloth folded over the back of a chair, just oilcloth spread for the family meal. What could he do with such a woman? He could not tell who was waiting for her or what she would eat for supper. He could not even guess at her name. She revealed nothing; would never help.

Grippes expelled the cats, shut the kitchen window, and dealt with the advance guard from behind the stove. What he needed now was despair and excitement, a new cat-and-mouse chase. What good was a computer that never caught anyone out?

After airing the kitchen and clearing it of poison, Grippes let the cats in. He swept up the bodies of his victims and sent them down the ancient cast-iron chute. He began to talk to himself, as he often did now. First he said a few sensible things, then he heard his voice with a new elderly quaver to it, virtuous and mean: "After all, it doesn't take much to keep me happy."

Now, that was untrue, and he had no reason to say it. Is that what I am going to be like, now, he wondered. Is this the new-era Grippes, pinch-mouthed? It was exactly the sort of thing that the woman in the dark dining room might say. The best thing that could happen to him would be shock, a siege of terror, a knock at the door and a registered letter with fearful news. It would sharpen his humor, strengthen his own, private, eccentric heart. It would keep him from making remarks in his solitude that were meaningless and false. He could perhaps write an anonymous letter saying that the famous author Henri Grippes was guilty of evasion of a most repulsive kind. He was, moreover, a callous landlord who had never been known to replace a doorknob. Fortunately, he saw, he was not yet that mad, nor did he really need to be scared and obsessed. He had got the woman from church to dining room, and he would keep her there, trapped, cornered, threatened, watched, until she yielded to Grippes and told her name—as, in his several incarnations, good Poche had always done.

A RECOLLECTION

I married Magdalena here, in Paris, more than forty years ago. It was at the time when anti-Jewish thoughts and feelings had suddenly hardened into laws, and she had to be protected. She was a devout, light-hearted, probably wayward Catholic convert, of the sort Dominicans like to have tea with, but she was also Jewish and foreign—to be precise, born in Budapest, in 1904. A Frenchman who had grown rich manufacturing and exporting fine china brought her to Paris—oh, a long time ago, even before the Popular Front. He gave her up for the daughter of a count, and for his new career in right-wing politics, preaching moral austerity and the restoration of Christian values. Whenever Magdalena opened *Le Temps* and saw his name, she would burst out laughing. (I never noticed Magdalena actually *reading* a newspaper. She subscribed to a great many, but I think it was just to see what her friends and former friends were up to.) He let her keep the apartment on Quai Voltaire and the van Dongen portraits he'd bought because they looked like her—the same pert face and slender throat.

I never lived with Magdalena. After our wedding we spent part of a week together (to calm my parents down, I went home to sleep) and a night sitting up in a train. I never imagined sharing an address, my name over the doorbell, friends calling me at Magdalena's number, myself any more than a guest in the black-red-and-white-lacquered apartment on Quai Voltaire. The whole place smelled of gardenias. Along the hall hung stills from films she had worked in, in Vienna, Berlin—silent, minor, forgotten pictures, probably all destroyed. (The apartment was looted during the Occupation. When Magdalena came back, she had to sleep on the floor.) Her two pug dogs yapped and wore little chimes. The constant jangling drove them crazy. She washed them with scented soap and fed them at table, sitting on her lap. They had rashes all over their bodies, and were always throwing up.

I was twenty-two, still a student. My parents, both teachers in the lower grades, had made great sacrifices so that I could sit reading books into early manhood. The only home I could have offered Magdalena was a corner of their flat, in the Rue des Solitaires, up in the Nineteenth Arrondissement. Arabs and Africans live there now. In those days, it was the kind of district Jean Renoir and René Clair liked to use for those films that show chimney pots, and people walking around with loaves of bread, and gentle young couples that find and lose a winning lottery ticket. Until she met me, Magdalena had never heard of the Rue des Solitaires, or of my Métro stop, Place des Fêtes. The names sounded so charming that she thought I'd made them up. I begged her to believe that I never invented anything.

She was fair and slight, like all the women in Paris. In my view of the past, the streets are filled with blond-haired women, wearing absurd little hats, walking miniature dogs. (Wait, my memory tells me; not all women—not my mother.) Why had she given up acting? "Because I wasn't much good," she told me once. "And I was so lazy. I could work, really work, for a man in love with me—to do him a favor. That was all." From her sitting room, everything in it white, you saw across the Seine to the

Place du Carrousel and part of the Tuileries. Between five and eight, men used to drop in, stand about with their backs to the view, lean down to scratch the ears of the pugs. Raymonde, the maid, knew everyone by name. They treated me kindly, though nobody ever went so far as to scratch my ears.

My parents were anticlerical and republican. In their conversation, Church and Republic locked horns like a couple of battling rams. I was never baptized. It broke their hearts that my marriage to Magdalena had to be blessed, at her insistence. The blessing was given in the church of Saint-Thomas-d'Aquin, in deep shadow, somewhere behind the altar. I had never been in a church before, except to admire windows or paintings; art belonged to the people, whatever the Vatican claimed. The ceremony was quick, almost furtive, but not because of Magdalena: *I* was the outsider, the pagan, unbaptized, unsaved.

My father and mother stayed home that day, eating the most solid lunch they could scrape together, to steady their nerves. They would have saved Magdalena, if only someone had asked— gladly, bravely, and without ruining my life. (That was how they saw it.) I suppose they could have locked her up in the broom closet. She could have stood in the dark, for years and years—as many as she needed. They could only hope, since they never prayed, that there would be no children.

I had already signed our children over to Rome a few days before the wedding, one afternoon just after lunch. Bargaining for their souls, uncreated, most certainly unwished for (I did not separate soul from body, since the first did not exist), went on in the white sitting room. Magdalena, as ever blithe and light-hearted, repeated whatever she'd been told to tell me, and I said yes, and signed. I can still hear the sound of her voice, though not the words she used; it was lower in pitch than a Frenchwoman's, alien to the ear because of its rhythm. It was a voice that sang a foreign song. Did she really expect to have children? She must have been thirty-six, and we were about to be separated for as long as the war might last. My signature was part of an elaborate ritual, in which she seemed to take immense delight. She had never been married before.

She had on a soft navy-blue dress, which had only that morning been brought to the door. This in war, in defeat. There were dressmakers and deliverymen. There was Chanel's Gardenia. There was coffee and sugar, there were polished silver trays and thin coffee cups. There was Raymonde, in black with white organdie, and Magdalena, with her sunny hair, her deep-red nails, to pour.

I looked over at the far side of the Place du Carrousel, to some of the windows of the Ministry of Finance. Until just a few months ago, Magdalena had been invited to private Ministry apartments to lunch. The tables were set with the beautiful glass and china that belonged to the people. Steadfast, uncomplaining men and women like my father and mother had paid their taxes so that Magdalena could lunch off plates they would never see— unless some further revolution took place, after which they might be able to view the plates in a museum.

I felt no anger thinking this. It was Magdalena I intended to save. As my wife, she would have an identity card with a French name. She would never have to baste a yellow star on her coat. She would line up for potatoes at a decent hour once France had run out of everything else.

Actually, Magdalena never lined up for anything. On the day when the Jews of Paris stood in long queues outside police stations, without pushing and shoving, and spelled their names and addresses clearly, so that the men coming to arrest them later on would not make a mistake, Magdalena went back to bed and read magazines. Nobody ever offered her a yellow star, but she found one for herself. It was lying on the ground, in front of the entrance to the Hôtel Meurice—so she said.

Walking the pugs in the rain, Magdalena had looked back to wave at Raymonde, polishing a window. (A publisher of comic books has the place now.) She crossed the Tuileries, then the

Rue de Rivoli, and, stepping under the arcades, furled her silk umbrella. Rain had driven in; she skirted puddles in her thin shoes. Just level with the Meurice, where there were so many German officers that some people were afraid to walk there, or scorned to, she stopped to examine a star—soiled, trodden on. She moved it like a wet leaf with the point of her umbrella, bent, picked it up, dropped it in her purse.

"Why?" I had good reason to ask, soon after.

"To keep as a souvenir, a curiosity. To show my friends in Cannes, so that they can see what things are like in Paris."

I didn't like that. I had wanted to pull her across to my side, not to be dragged over to hers.

A day later we set off by train for the South, which was still a free zone. The only Nazis she would be likely to encounter there would be French; I gave Magdalena a lecture on how to recognize and avoid them. We sat side by side in a second-class compartment, in the near dark. (Much greater suspicion attended passengers in first; besides that, I could not afford it.) Magdalena, unfortunately, was dressed for tea at the Ritz. She would have retorted that nothing could be plainer than a Molyneux suit and a diamond pin. The other passengers, three generations of a single family, seemed to be asleep. On the new, unnatural frontier dividing France North from South, the train came to a halt. We heard German soldiers coming on board, to examine our papers. Trying not to glance at Magdalena, I fixed my eyes on the small overnight case she had just got down from the rack and sat holding on her lap. When the train stopped, all the lights suddenly blazed—seemed to blaze; they were dull and brown. Magdalena at once stood up, got her case down without help, removed a novel (it was *Bella*, by Jean Giraudoux), and began to read.

I thought that she had done the very thing bound to make her

seem suspect. Her past, intricate and inscrutable, was summed
up by the rich leather of the case and the gold initials on the lid
and the tiny gold padlock and key, in itself a piece of jewelry.
That woman could not possibly be the wife of that young man,
with his rolled-up canvas holdall with the cracked leather straps.
The bag was not even mine; it had belonged to my mother, or an
aunt. I reached over and turned her case around, so that I could
open it, as if I were anxious to co-operate, to get things ready for
inspection. The truth was, I did not want the German peasants in
uniform to read her initials, to ask what her maiden name was, or
to have cause for envy; the shut case might have been offered for
sale in a window along the Rue du Faubourg-Saint-Honoré, at
extortionate cost. I thought that if those peasants, now approach-
ing our compartment, had not been armed, booted, temporarily
privileged, they might have served a different apprenticeship—
learned to man mirror-walled elevators, carry trays at shoulder
level, show an underling's gratitude for Magdalena's escort's tip.
I flung the lid back, against her jacket of thin wool; and there,
inside, on top of some folded silk things the color of the palest
edge of sunrise, lay a harsh star. I smoothed the silken stuff and
palmed the star and got it up my sleeve.

In my terrible fright my mind caught on something inciden-
tal—that Magdalena had never owned anything else so coarse to
the touch. She had never been a child, had never played with
sand and mud. She had been set down in a large European city,
smart hat tilted, rings swivelled so that she could pull her gloves
on, knowing all there is about gold padlocks and keys. "Cosmopolitan," an incendiary word now, flared in my mind. In the
quiet train (no train is so still as one under search), its light
seemed to seek out crude editorials, offensive cartoons, repulsive
graffiti.

The peasants in uniform—they were two—slid open the
compartment door. They asked no more than any frontier
inspector, but the reply came under the heading of life and death.
"Cosmopolitan" had flared like a star; it dissolved into a dirty

little puddle. Its new, political meaning seeped into my brain and ran past my beliefs and convictions, and everything my parents stood for. I felt it inside my skull, and I wondered if it would ever evaporate.

One of the peasants spoke, and Magdalena smiled. She told me later that he had the accent said to have been Wagner's. Seeing the open case, he plunged his hand under the silks and struck a hairbrush. He shut the lid and stared dumbly at the initials. The other one in the meanwhile frowned at our papers. Then the pair of them stumbled out.

Our fellow-passengers looked away, as people do when someone with the wrong ticket is caught in first class. I put the case back on the rack and muttered an order. Magdalena obediently followed me out to the corridor. It may have looked as if we were just standing, smoking, but I was trying to find out how she, who had never owned anything ugly, had come into possession of this thing. She told me about the Rue de Rivoli, and that she had thought the star would interest her friends in Cannes: they would be able to see how things were now up in Paris. If she had buried it next to her hairbrush, it would have seemed as though she had something to hide. She said she had nothing to hide; absolutely nothing.

I had been running with sweat; now I felt cold. I asked her if she was crazy. She took this for the anxious inquiry of a young man deeply in love. Her nature was sunny, and as good as gold. She laughed and told me she had been called different things but never crazy. She started to repeat some of them, and I kissed her to shut her up. The corridor was jammed with people lying sprawled or sitting on their luggage, and she sounded demented and foreign.

I wondered what she meant by "friends in Cannes." To women of her sort, "friend" is often used as a vague substitute for "lover." (Notice how soon after thinking "cosmopolitan" I thought "of her sort.") She had mentioned the name of the people who were offering her shelter in Cannes; it was a French

name but perhaps an alias. I had a right to know more. She was
my wife. For the first and the last time I considered things in that
particular way: After all, she *is* my wife. I was leaving the train at
Marseilles, though my ticket read Cannes. From Marseilles, I
would try to get to North Africa, then to England. Magdalena
would sit the war out in an airy villa—the kind aliens can afford.

When I next said something—about getting back to our
seats—my voice was too high. It still rises and thins when I feel
under strain. (In the nineteen-fifties, when I was often heard over
the radio, interviewing celebrated men about their early struggles
and further ambitions, I would get about two letters a year from
women saying they envied my mother.)

It was probably just as well that we were spending our last night
among strangers. After our wedding we had almost ceased to be
lovers. I had to keep the peace at home, and Magdalena to
prepare to leave without showing haste. I thought she was tense
and tired; but I appreciate now that Magdalena was never
fatigued or wrought up, and I can only guess she had to say
goodbye to someone else. She sent the dogs away to Raymonde's
native town in Normandy, mentioning to the concierge that it
was for the sake of their health and for a few days only. At the first
sign of fright, of hurry, or of furniture removed to storage, the
concierge might have been halfway to the police station to report
on the tenant who had so many good friends, and whose voice
sang a foreign tune.

In the compartment, I tried to finish the thoughts begun in the
corridor. I had married her to do the right thing; that was
established. Other men have behaved well in the past, and will
continue to do so. It comforted me to know I was not the only
one with a safe conscience. Thinking this in the darkened,
swaying compartment meant that I was lucid and generous, and
also something of a louse. I whispered to Magdalena, "What is
bad behavior? What is the worst?" The question did not seem to
astonish her. Our union was blessed, and she was my wife
forevermore, and she could fall back on considerable jurispru-

dence from the ledgers of Heaven to prove it; but I was still the student who had brought his books to Quai Voltaire, who had looked up to make sure she was still in the room, and asked some question from beyond his experience. She took my hand and said the worst *she* remembered was the Viennese novelist who had taken some of her jewelry (she meant "stolen") and pawned it and kept all the money.

We said goodbye in Marseilles, on the station platform. In the southern morning light her eyes were pale blue. There were armed men in uniform everywhere. She wore a white suit and a thin blouse and a white hat I had never seen before. She had taken a suitcase into the filthy toilet and emerged immaculate. I had the feeling that she could hardly wait to get back on the train and roll on to new adventures.

"And now I am down here, away from all my friends in Paris," she had the gall to say, shading her eyes. It was a way of showing spirit, but I had never known anyone remotely like her, and I probably thought she should be tight-lipped. By "all my friends" she must have meant men who had said, "If you ever need help," knowing she would never ask; who might have said, "Wasn't it awful, tragic, about Magdalena?" if she had never been seen again.

She had left her luggage and jewelry untended in the compartment. I was glad to see she wore just her wedding ring; otherwise, she might have looked too actressy, and drawn attention. (I had no idea how actresses were supposed to look.) Sometimes she used an amber cigarette holder with a swirl of diamond dust like the tail of a comet. She must have sold it during the war; or perhaps lost it, or given it away.

"You look like a youth leader," she said. I was Paris-pale, but healthy. My hair was clipped short. I might have been about to lead police and passengers in patriotic singsong. I was patriotic, but not as the new regime expected its young to be; I was on my way to be useful to General de Gaulle, if he would have me. I saw myself floating over the map of France, harnessed to a dazzling parachute, with a gun under my arm.

We had agreed not to stare at each other once we'd said goodbye. Magdalena kissed me and turned and pulled herself up the high steps of the train. I got a soft, bent book out of my canvas holdall and began to read something that spoke only to me. So the young think, and I was still that young: poetry is meant for one reader only. Magdalena, gazing tenderly down from the compartment window, must have seen just the shape of the poem on the page. I turned away from the slant of morning sunlight— not away from her. When the train started to move, she reached down to me, but I was too far to touch. A small crucifix on a chain slipped free of her blouse. I stuck to our promise and never once raised my eyes. At the same time, I saw everything—the shade of her white hatbrim aslant on her face, her hand with the wedding ring.

I put the star in my book, to mark the place: I figured that if I was caught I was done for anyway. When my adventures were over, I would show it to my children; I did not for a second see Magdalena as their mother. They were real children, not souls to be bargained. So it seems to me now. It shows how far into the future I thought you could safely carry a piece of the past. Long after the war, I found the star, still in the same book, and I offered to give it back to Magdalena, but she said she knew what it was like.

RUE DE LILLE

My second wife, Juliette, died in the apartment on Rue de Lille, where she had lived—at first alone, more or less, then with me—since the end of the war. All the rooms gave onto the ivy-hung well of a court, and were for that reason dark. We often talked about looking for a brighter flat, on a top floor with southern exposure and a wide terrace, but Parisians seldom move until they're driven to. "We know the worst of what we've got," we told each other. "It's better than a bad surprise."

"And what about your books?" Juliette would add. "It would take you months to get them packed, and in the new place you'd never get them sorted." I would see myself as Juliette saw me, crouched over a slanting, shaking stack of volumes piled on a strange floor, cursing and swearing as I tried to pry out a dictionary. "Just the same, I don't intend to die here," she also said.

I once knew someone who believed drowning might be easy, even pleasant, until he almost drowned by accident. Juliette's father was a colonel who expected to die in battle or to be shot by a German firing squad, but he died of typhus in a concentration camp. I had once, long ago, imagined for myself a clandestine burial with full honors after some Resistance feat, but all I got out of the war was a few fractures and a broken nose in a motorcycle accident.

Juliette had thirty-seven years of blacked-out winter mornings in Rue de Lille. She was a few days short of her sixtieth birthday when I found her stretched out on the floor of our bedroom, a hand slackened on a flashlight. She had been trying to see under a chest of drawers, and her heart stopped. (Later, I pulled the chest away from the wall and discovered a five-franc coin.) Her gray-and-dark hair, which had grown soft and wayward with age, was tied back with a narrow satin ribbon. She looked more girlish than at any time since I'd first met her. (She fell in love with me young.) She wore a pleated flannel skirt, a tailored blouse, and one of the thick cardigans with gilt buttons she used to knit while watching television. She had been trained to believe that to look or to listen quietly is to do nothing; she would hum along with music, to show she wasn't idle. She was discreet, she was generous to a sensible degree, she was anything but contentious. I often heard her remark, a trifle worriedly, that she was never bored. She was faithful, if "faithful" means avoiding the acknowledged forms of trouble. She was patient. I know she was good. Any devoted male friend, any lover, any husband would have shown up beside her as selfish, irritable, even cruel. She displayed so little of the ordinary kinds of jealousy, the plain marital do-you-often-have-lunch-with-her? sort, that I once asked her if she had a piece missing.

"Whoever takes this place over," she said, when we spoke of moving, "will be staggered by the size of the electricity bills." (Juliette paid them; I looked after a number of other things.) We had to keep the lights turned on all day in winter. The apartment was L-shaped, bent round two sides of a court, like a train making a sharp turn. From our studies, at opposite ends of the train, we could look out and see the comforting glow of each other's working life, a lamp behind a window. Juliette would be giving some American novel a staunch, steady translation; I might be getting into shape my five-hour television series, "Stendhal and the Italian Experience," which was to win an award in Japan.

We were together for a duration of time I daren't measure against the expanse of Juliette's life; it would give me the feeling that I had decamped to a height of land, a survivor's eminence, so as to survey the point at which our lives crossed and mingled and began to move in the same direction: a long, narrow reach of time in the Rue de Lille. It must be the washy, indefinite colorations of blue that carpeted, papered, and covered floors, walls, and furniture and shaded our lamps which cast over that reach the tone of a short season. I am thinking of the patches of distant, neutral blue that appear over Paris in late spring, when it is still wet and cold in the street and tourists have come too early. The tourists shelter in doorways, trying to read their soaked maps, perennially unprepared in their jeans and thin jackets. Overhead, there are scrapings of a color that carries no threat and promises all.

That choice, Juliette's preference, I sometimes put down to her Calvinist sobriety—call it a temperament—and sometimes to a refinement of her Huguenot taste. When I was feeling tired or impatient, I complained that I had been consigned to a Protestant Heaven by an arbitrary traffic cop, and that I was better suited to a pagan Hell. Again, as I looked round our dining-room table at the calm, clever faces of old friends of Juliette's family, at their competent and unassuming wives, I saw what folly it might be to set such people against a background of buttercup yellow or apple green. The soft clicking of their upper-class Protestant consonants made conversation distant and neutral, too. It was a voice that had puzzled me the first time I'd heard it from Juliette. I had supposed, mistakenly, that she was trying it on for effect; but she was wholly natural.

The sixteenth-century map of Paris I bought for her birthday is still at the framer's; I sent a check but never picked it up. I destroyed her private correspondence without reading it, and gave armfuls of clothes away to a Protestant charity. To the personal notice of her death in *Le Monde* was attached a brief mention of her father, a hero of the Resistance for whom suburban streets are named; and of her career as a respected translator, responsible for having introduced postwar American literature to French readers; and of her husband, the well-known radio and television interviewer and writer, who survived her.

Another person to survive her was my first wife. One night when Juliette and I were drinking coffee in the little sitting room where she received her women friends, and where we watched television, Juliette said, again, "But how much of what she says does she believe? About her Catholicism, and all those fantasies running round in her head—that she is your true and only wife, that your marriage is registered in Heaven, that you and she will be together in another world?"

"Those are things people put in letters," I said. "They sit down alone and pour it out. It's sincere at that moment. I don't know why she would suddenly be *in*sincere."

"After all the trouble she's made," said Juliette. She meant that for many years my wife would not let me divorce.

"She couldn't help that," I said.

"How do you know?"

"I don't know. It's what I think. I hardly knew her."

"You must have known *something*."

"I haven't seen her more than three or four times in the last thirty-odd years, since I started living with you."

"What do you mean?" said Juliette. "You saw her just once, with me. We had lunch. You backed off asking for the divorce."

"You can't ask for a divorce at lunch. It had to be done by mail."

"And since then she hasn't stopped writing," said Juliette. "Do you mean three or four times, or do you mean once?"

I said, "Once, probably. Probably just that once."

Viewing me at close range, as if I were a novel she had to translate, Juliette replied that one ought to be spared unexpected visions. Just now, it was as if three walls of the court outside had been bombed flat. Through a bright new gap she saw straight through to my first marriage. We—my first wife and I—postured in the distance, like characters in fiction.

I had recently taken part in a panel discussion, taped for television, on the theme "What Literature, for Which Readers, at Whose Price?" I turned away from Juliette and switched on the set, about ten minutes too early. Juliette put the empty cups and the coffeepot on a tray she had picked up in Milan, the summer I was researching the Stendhal, and carried the tray down the dim passage to the kitchen. I watched the tag end of the late news. It must have been during the spring of 1976. Because of the energy crisis, daylight saving had been established. Like any novelty, it was deeply upsetting. People said they could no longer digest their food or be nice to their children, and that they needed sedation to help them through the altered day. A doctor was interviewed; he advised a light diet and early bed until mind and body adjusted to the change.

I turned, smiling, to where Juliette should have been. My program came on then, and I watched myself making a few points before I got up and went to find her. She was in the kitchen, standing in the dark, clutching the edge of the sink. She did not move when I turned the light on. I put my arms around her, and we came back to her sitting room and watched the rest of the program together. She was knitting squares of wool to be sewn together to make a blanket; there was always, somewhere, a flood or an earthquake or a flow of refugees, and those who outlasted jeopardy had to be covered.

THE COLONEL'S CHILD

I got to London by way of Marseilles and North Africa, having left Paris more than a year before. My aim was to join the Free French and General de Gaulle. I believed the weight of my presence could tip the scales of war, like one vote in a close election. There was no vanity in this. London was the peak of my hopes and desires. I could look back and see a tamed landscape. My past life dwindled and vanished in that long perspective. I was twenty-three.

In my canvas hold-all I carried a tobacco pouch someone had given me, filled with thin reddish soil from Algeria. In those days earth from France and earth from Algeria meant the same thing. Only years later was I able to think, I must have been crazy. When you are young, your patriotism is like metaphysical frenzy. Later, it becomes one more aspect of personal crankiness.

Instead of a hero's welcome I was given forms to fill out. These questionnaires left no room for postscripts, and so only a skeleton of myself could be drawn. I was Édouard B., born in Paris, father a schoolteacher (so was my mother, but I wasn't asked), student of literature and philosophy, single, no dependents.

Some definitions seemed incomplete. For instance, I was not

entirely single: before leaving Paris I had married a Jewish-born actress, so as to give her the security of my name. As far as I knew, she was now safe and in Cannes. At the same time, I was not a married man. The marriage was an incident, gradually being rubbed out in the long perspective I've described. So I saw it; so I would insist. You have to remember the period, and France occupied, to imagine how one could think and behave. We always say this—"Think of the times we had to live in"—when the past is dragged forward, all the life gone out of it, and left unbreathing at our feet.

Instead of sending me off to freeze on a parade ground, the Free French kept me in London. I took it to mean they wanted to school me in sabotage work and drop me into France. I did not know special parachute training might be needed. I thought you held your breath and jumped.

Two months later I lay in a hospital ward with a broken nose, broken left arm, and fractures in both legs. They had been trying to teach me to ride a motorbike, and on my first time out I skidded into a wall. The instructor came and sat by my bedside. He was about twice my age, a former policeman from Rouen. He said the Free French weren't quite casting me off, but some of them wondered if I was meant for a fighting force in exile. I was a cerebral type, who needed the peace of an office job, with no equipment to smash—not even a typewriter. I asked if General de Gaulle had been informed about my accident.

"Is he a friend of yours?" said the instructor.

"I've seen him," I said. "I saw him in Carlton Gardens. He came out the door and down some steps, and got into his car. I was carrying a lot of parcels, so I couldn't salute. I don't think he noticed. I hope not."

There was a silence, during which the instructor stared at his watch. Presently, he inquired what I wanted to do with my life.

"I think I am a poet," I said. "I can't be sure."

After that they sent me a regular hospital visitor, a volunteer. Juliette was her name. She was seventeen, from Bordeaux, the daughter of a colonel who had followed de Gaulle to London.

She had a precise, particular way of speaking, with every syllable given full value and the consonants treated like little stones. It was not the native accent of Bordeaux, which anyone can imitate, or the everyday French of Paris I'd grown up with, but the tone, almost undefinable, of the French Protestant upper class. I had not heard it before, not consciously, and for the moment had no means of placing it. I thought she had picked up an affectation of some sort while learning English and had carried it over to French. She had, besides, the habit of thrusting into French conversation brief, joyous, and usually irrelevant remarks in English: "You don't say!" "Oh, what a shame!" "How glad I am for you!" "How gorgeous!"

From behind a mask of splints and bandages I appraised her face, which was still childlike, rounded as if over a layer of cream. A beret kept slipping and sliding off her dark hair. "Oh, what a pity!" she remarked, pulling it back on. She was dressed in the least becoming clothes I had ever seen on a young woman—a worn and drooping tunic, thick black stockings, and a navy sweater frayed at the cuffs. She had spent five months in an English girls' school, she told me, and this was the remains of a uniform. She had nothing else to wear, nothing that fitted. Her mother was too busy to shop.

"Can't you shop for yourself?"

"It's not done," she said. "I mean, we don't do things that way."

"Who is we?"—for she still puzzled me.

"Besides, I've got no money." This seemed a sensible explanation. I wondered why she had bothered to make another. "My mother teaches English to French recruits. Actually, she doesn't know much, but she can make them read traffic signs."

"You mean, 'Stop'?"

"Well, there are other things—'No Entry.'" She looked troubled, as if she were not succeeding in the tranquil, sleepy conversation that is supposed to keep a victim's mind off his wounds.

I had lost six front teeth in the accident. Through the gap, Juliette fed me the mess the English call custard. My right arm was fine, but I let her do it. She was grave, intent—a little girl playing. She might have been poking a spoon into a doll's porcelain face. When I refused to swallow any more, she got a bottle of eau de cologne and a facecloth out of a satchel and carefully wiped my hands and wrists and around my neck— whatever was bare and visible. I wondered if she would offer to comb my hair and cut my nails, but the nursing part of the game was over. She sat with her ankles crossed and her hands clasped, a good girl on a visit, and told me that her father, the colonel, was an outcast with a price on his head. From the care she took not to say where he was, I understood they had sent him to France, on a mission. Forgetting about secrets, she suddenly said she yearned to be smuggled into France, too, so that she could join him and they might blow up bridges together.

"I wanted to do that," I said. "That's why I came here. But I'm useless. I may come out of this with a scarred face, or a limp. I'd be at risk."

"Oh, I know," said Juliette. "The Germans would catch you and shoot you. They'd look for a secret agent all covered with scars. Oh, what a nuisance!"

Sweet Juliette. Her dark eyes held all the astonished eagerness of a child of twelve. I often think I should want to be back there, with a Juliette still virginal, untouched, saying encouraging things such as "all covered with scars," but at the age I am now it would bore me.

She came to the hospital twice a week, then every day. Her mother was at work, and I felt the girl had time on her hands and was often lonely. She was with me when they took the last of the mask off. "Well?" I said. "Tell me the worst."

"I can't," she said. "I don't know how you were before." She held up a pocket mirror. My nose was broken, all right, and I had thick, bruised cheekbones, like a Cossack. For someone who had never been to war, I was amazingly the image of an old soldier.

I left the hospital on crutches. There was no such thing as
therapy—you got going or you did not. The organization
found me a room on Baker Street, not far from where Juliette
lived with her mother, as it turned out, and they gave me low-
grade and harmless work to do. As my instructor had predicted, I
was let nowhere near a typewriter, and once, I remember,
someone even snatched a pencil sharpener away. Juliette used to
come to the office, though she wasn't supposed to, and sit by my
desk as if it were a bed. She had got rid of the uniform, but her
new clothes, chosen by her mother, were English and baggy, in
the grays and mustards Englishwomen favored. They seemed
picked deliberately to make her creamy skin sallow, her slender-
ness gaunt. The mother was keeping her plain, I thought,
perhaps to keep her out of trouble. Why didn't Juliette rebel? She
was eighteen by now, but forty years ago eighteen was young. I
wondered why she hung around me, what she wanted. I thought
I guessed, but I decided not to know. I didn't want it said I had
destroyed two items of French property—a motorcycle and a
colonel's child. It was here, in London, that I was starting to get
the hang of French society. In our reduced world, everyone in it
a symbol of native, inborn rank, Juliette stood higher than some
random young man who had merely laid his life on the line. She
had connections, simply by the nature of how things were
ordered.

I asked her once if there was a way of getting a message to my
mother, in Paris—just a word to say I was safe. She pretended not
to hear but about a month later said, "No, it's too dangerous.
Besides, they don't trust you."

"Don't trust me? Why not?"

"I'm not sure."

"Do you?" I said.

"That's different."

Her mother was out most evenings. When Juliette was alone, I
brought my rations around, and she cooked our supper. We
drank—only because everybody did—replacing the whiskey in

her mother's precious Haig bottle with London tap water. Once, Juliette tried restoring the color with cold tea, and there was hell to pay. When the news came from France that her father had been arrested and identified, she came straight to me.

"I'll never see him again," she said. "I haven't even got a decent snapshot of him. My mother has them all. She's got them in a suitcase. I feel sick. Feel my forehead. Feel my cheeks." She took my hand. "Feel the back of my neck. Feel my throat," she said, dragging my hand. We left the office and went to her flat and pulled the blackout curtain. The sun was shining on the other side of the street, where everything was bombed, but she didn't want to see it.

"How do you know your mother's not going to walk in?" I said. "She may want to be alone with you. She may want a quiet place to cry."

Juliette shook her head. "We're not like that. We don't do those things."

I think of the love and despair she sent out to me, the young shoots wild and blind, trusting me for support. She asked me to tell my most important secret, so that we would be bound. The most intimate thing I could say was that I was writing less poetry and had started a merciless novel about the French in London.

"I could tell you a lot," said Juliette. "Heroes' wives sleeping with other men."

"It's not that sort of novel," I said. "In my novel, they're all dead, but they don't know it. Every character is in a special Hell, made to measure."

"That's not how it is," she said. "We're not dead or in Hell. We're just here, waiting. We don't know what Hell will be like. Nobody knows. And some of us are going to be together in Heaven." She put her face against mine, saying this. It never occurred to me that she meant it, literally. I thought her Calvinism was just an organized form of disbelief. "Haven't you got some better secret?" she said. I supposed that schoolgirls talked this way, pledging friendship, and I wondered what she was taking me for. "Well," she said presently, "will you marry me anyway, even without a secret?"

Nobody coerced me into a life with Juliette. There were no tears, no threats, and I was not afraid of her mother. All I had to say was "I don't know yet" or "We'll see." I think I wanted to get her out of her loneliness. When for all her shyness she asked if I loved her, I said I would never leave her, and I am sure we both thought it meant the same thing. A few days later she told her mother that we were engaged and that nothing would keep her from marrying me after the war, and, for the first time since she could remember, she saw her mother cry.

Instead of a ring I gave Juliette some of the Algerian soil. She thanked me but confessed she had no idea what to do with it. Should it be displayed in a saucer, on a low table? Should she seal it up in a labelled, dated envelope? Tactful from infancy, she offered the gift to her mother, her rival in grief.

Now that we were "engaged," I began to see what the word covered for Juliette, and I had no qualms about smuggling her into my room—though never, of course, late at night. We took the mattress off the sagging daybed and put it on the floor, in front of the gas fire. Juliette would take her clothes off and tell me about her early years, though I didn't always listen. Sometimes she talked about the life waiting for us in Paris, and the number of children we would have, and the names we would give them. I remember a Thomas and a Claire.

"How many children should we have?" she said. "I'd say about ten. Well, seven. At least five."

Her clothes were scattered all over the floor, and the room was cold, in spite of the fire, but she didn't seem to feel it. "I hate children," I said. I was amazed that I could say something so definite and so cruel, and that sounded so true. When had I stopped liking them? Perhaps when I adopted the colonel's child, believing she would never grow up. I could have said, "I don't like *other* children," but nothing about this conversation was thought out.

"You will love them," she said happily. "You'll see." She held her spread fingers against the gas flame, counting off their names. Each finger stood for a greedy, willful personality, as tough as a fist. An only child, she invented playmates and named them, and I was supposed to bring them to life.

"I know it sounds stupid," she said, "but I kept my dolls until I was fifteen. My mother finally gave them away."

"Brothers and sisters," I said.

"No, just dolls. But they did have names."

"Is that one of your secrets?" "Secrets" had become charged with erotic meaning, when we were alone.

"You've got a special secret," she said.

"Yes. I've torn up my novel."

"Oh, how lovely for you! Or is that sad?"

"I'm just giving it up. I'll never start another."

"You've got another secret," she said. "You're married to someone." As she said this, she seemed to become aware that the room was cold. She shivered and reached for her dress, and drew it around her like a shawl. "A person went to see your mother. She—your mother—said to tell you your wife was all right. Your *wife*," said Juliette, trying to control her voice, "is in the South of France. She has managed to send your mother a pound of onions. To eat," said Juliette, as I went on staring. "Onions, to eat."

"I did get married," I said. "But she's not my wife. I did it to save her. I've got her yellow star somewhere."

"I'd like to see it," said Juliette, politely.

"It is made of cheap, ugly material," I said, as if that were the only thing wrong.

"I think you should put some clothes on," said Juliette. "If you're going to tell about your wife."

"She isn't my wife," I said. "The marriage was just something legal. Apart from being legal, it doesn't count."

"She may not be your wife," said Juliette, "but she is your mother's daughter-in-law." She drew up her knees and bent her head on them, as if it were disgraceful to watch me dressing. "You mean," she said, after a time, "that it doesn't count as a secret?" I gathered up the rest of her clothes and put them beside her on the mattress. "Does it count as anything?"

"I'll walk you home," I said.

"You don't need to."

"It's late. I can't have you wandering around in the blackout."

She dressed, slowly, sitting and kneeling. "I am glad she is safe and well," she said. "It would be too bad if you had done all that for nothing. She must be very grateful to you."

I had never thought about gratitude. It seemed to me that, yes, she was probably grateful. I suddenly felt impatient for the war to end, so that I could approach her, hand in hand with Juliette, and ask for a divorce and a blessing.

Juliette, kneeling, fastened the buttons of the latest flour sack her mother had chosen. "Why did you tear up your novel?" she said.

Because I can't wrench life around to make it fit some fantasy. Because I don't know how to make life sound worse or better, or how to make it sound true. Instead of saying this, I said, "How do you expect me to support ten children?" The colonel's wife didn't like me much, but she had said that after the war there were a few people she could introduce me to. She had mentioned something about radio broadcasting, and I liked the idea. Juliette was still kneeling, with only part of the hideous dress buttoned up. I looked down at her bent head. She must have been thinking that she had tied herself to a man with no money, no prospects, and no connections. Who wasn't entirely single. Who might be put on a charge for making a false declaration. Who had a broken nose and a permanent limp. Who, so far, had never finished anything he'd started. Perhaps she was forgetting one thing: I had got to London.

"I could stay all night," she said. "If you want me to."

"Your mother would have the police out," I said.

"She'd never dare," said Juliette. "I've never called the police because *she* didn't come home."

"It would be..." I tried to think of what it could be for us. "It would be radical."

Her hands began to move again, the other way, unbuttoning. She was the colonel's child, she had already held her breath and jumped, and that was the start and the end of it.

"We may be in big trouble over this," I said.

"Oh, what a pity," she said. "We'll always be together. We will always be happy. How lovely! What a shame!"

I think she still trusted me at that moment; I hope so.

LENA

In her prime, by which I mean in her beauty, my first wife,
Magdalena, had no use for other women. She did not
depend upon women for anything that mattered, such as
charm and enjoyment and getting her bills paid; and as for
exchanging Paris gossip and intimate chitchat, since she never
confided anything personal and never complained, a man's ear
was good enough. Magdalena saw women as accessories, to be
treated kindly—maids, seamstresses, manicurists—or as comic
minor figures, the wives and official fiancées of her admirers. It
was not in her nature to care what anyone said, and she never
could see the shape of a threat even when it rolled over her, but I
suspect that she was called some of the senseless things she was
called, such as "Central European whore" and "Jewish adven-
turess," by women.

Now that she is nearly eighty and bedridden, she receives visits
from women—the residue of an early wave of Hungarian emigra-
tion. They have small pink noses, wear knitted caps pulled down
to their eyebrows, and can see on dark street corners the terrible
ghost of Béla Kun. They have forgotten that Magdalena once

seemed, perhaps, disreputable. She is a devout Catholic, and she says cultivated, moral-sounding things, sweet to the ears of half a dozen widows of generals and bereft sisters of bachelor diplomats. They crowd her bedside table with bottles of cough mixture, lemons, embroidered table napkins, jars of honey, and covered bowls of stewed plums, the juice from which always spills. They call Magdalena "Lena."

She occupies a bed in the only place that would have her—a hospital on the northern rim of Paris, the color of jails, daubed with graffiti. The glass-and-marble lobby commemorates the flashy prosperity of the nineteen-sixties. It contains, as well as a vandalized coffee machine and a plaque bearing the name of a forgotten Minister of Health, a monumental example of the art of twenty years ago: a white foot with each toenail painted a different color. In order to admire this marvel, and to bring Magdalena the small comforts I think she requires, I need to travel a tiring distance by the underground suburban train. On these expeditions I carry a furled umbrella: the flat, shadeless light of this line is said to attract violent crime. In my wallet I have a card attesting to my right to sit down, because of an accident suffered in wartime. I never dare show the card. I prefer to stand. Anything to do with the Second World War, particularly its elderly survivors, arouses derision and ribaldry and even hostility in the young.

Magdalena is on the fourth floor (no elevator) of a wing reserved for elderly patients too frail to be diverted to nursing homes—assuming that a room for her in any such place could be found. The old people have had it drummed into them that they are lucky to have a bed, that the waiting list for their mattress and pillow lengthens by the hour. They must not seem too capricious, or dissatisfied, or quarrelsome, or give the nurses extra trouble. If they persist in doing so, their belongings are packed and their relatives sent for. A law obliges close relatives to take them in. Law isn't love, and Magdalena has seen enough distress and confusion to make her feel thoughtful.

"Families are worse than total war," she says. I am not sure what her own war amounted to. As far as I can tell, she endured all its rigors in Cannes, taking a daily walk to a black-market restaurant, her legs greatly admired by famous collaborators and German officers along the way. Her memory, when she wants to be bothered with it, is like a brief, blurry, self-centered dream.

"But what were you *doing* during those years?" I have asked her. (My mother chalked Gaullist slogans on walls in Paris. The father of my second wife died deported. I joined the Free French in London.)

"I was holding my breath," she answers, smiling.

She shares a room with a woman who suffers from a burning rash across her shoulders. Medicine that relieves the burning seems to affect her mind, and she will wander the corridors, wondering where she is, weeping. The hospital then threatens to send her home, and her children, in a panic, beg that the treatment be stopped. After a few days the rash returns, and the woman keeps Magdalena awake describing the pain she feels—it is like being flogged with blazing nettles, she says. Magdalena pilfers tranquillizers and gets her to take them, but once she hit the woman with a pillow. The hospital became nasty, and I had to step in. Fortunately, the supervisor of the aged-and-chronic department had seen me on television, taking part in a literary game ("Which saint might Jean-Paul Sartre have wanted most to meet?"), and that helped our case.

Actually, Magdalena cannot be evicted—not just like that. She has no family, and nowhere to go. Her continued existence is seen by the hospital as a bit of a swindle. They accepted her in the first place only because she was expected to die quite soon, releasing the bed.

"**Y**our broken nose is a mistake," she said to me the other day. My face was damaged in the same wartime accident that is supposed to give me priority seating rights in public transport. "It lends you an air of desperate nerve, as if a Malraux hero had wandered into a modern novel and been tossed out on his face."

Now, this was hard on a man who had got up earlier than usual and bought a selection of magazines for Magdalena before descending to the suburban line, with its flat, worrying light. A man who had just turned sixty-five. Whose new bridge made him lisp. She talks the way she talked in the old days, in her apartment with the big windows and the sweeping view across the Seine. She used to wear white, and sit on a white sofa. There were patches of red in the room—her long fingernails and her lipstick, and the Legion of Honor on some admirer's lapel. She had two small, funny dogs whose eyes glowed red in the dusk.

"I heard you speaking just the other day," she went on. "You were most interesting about the way Gide always made the rounds of the bookstores to see how his work was selling. Actually, I think I told you that story."

"It couldn't have been just the other day," I said. "It sounds like a radio program I had in the nineteen-fifties."

"It couldn't have been you, come to think of it," she said. "The man lisped. I said to myself, 'It *might* be Édouard.'"

Her foreign way of speaking enchanted me when I was young. Now it sharpens my temper. Fifty years in France and she still cannot pronounce my name, "Édouard," without putting the stress on the wrong syllable and rolling the "r." "When you come to an 'r,'" I have told her, "keep your tongue behind your lower front teeth."

"It won't stay," she says. "It curls up. I am sorry." As if she cared. She will accept any amount of petulance shown by me, because she thinks she owes me tolerance: she sees me as youthful, boyish, to be teased and humored. She believes we have a long, unhampered life before us, and she expects to occupy it as my wife and widow-to-be. To that end, she has managed to outlive my second wife, and she may well survive me, even though I am fourteen years younger than she is and still on my feet.

Magdalena's Catholic legend is that she was converted after hearing Jacques Maritain explain Neo-Thomism at a tea party. Since then, she has never stopped heaping metaphysical rules about virtue on top of atavistic arguments concerning right and wrong. The result is a moral rock pile, ready to slide. Only God himself could stand up to the avalanche, but in her private arrangements he is behind her, egging her on. I had to wait until a law was passed that allowed divorce on the ground of separation before I was free to marry again. I waited a long time. In the meantime, Magdalena was writing letters to the Pope, cheering his stand on marriage and urging him to hold firm. She can choose among three or four different languages, her choice depending on where her dreams may have taken her during the night. She used to travel by train to Budapest and Prague wearing white linen. She had sleek, fair hair, and wore a diamond hair clip behind one ear. Now no one goes to those places, and the slim linen suits are crumpled in trunks. Her mind is clear, but she says absurd things. "I never saw her," she said about Juliette, my second wife. "Was she anything like me?"

"You did see her. We had lunch, the three of us."

"Show me her picture. It might bring back the occasion."

"No."

They met, once, on the first Sunday of September, 1954—a hot day of quivering horizons and wasps hitting the windshield. I had a new Renault—a model with a reputation for rolling over and lying with its wheels in the air. I drove, I think, grimly. Magdalena was beside me, in a nimbus of some scent—jasmine, or gardenia—that made me think of the opulent, profiteering side of wars. Juliette sat behind, a road map on her knee, her finger on the western outskirts of Fontainebleau. Her dark hair was pulled back tight and tied at the nape of her neck with a dark-blue grosgrain ribbon. It is safe to say that she smelled of soap and lemons.

We were taking Magdalena out to lunch. It was Juliette's idea. Somewhere between raspberries-and-cream and coffee, I was supposed to ask for a divorce—worse, to coax from Magdalena the promise of collusion in obtaining one. So far, she had resisted any mention of the subject and for ten years had refused to see me. Juliette and I had been living together since the end of the war. She was thirty now, and tired of waiting. We were turning into one of those uneasy, shadowy couples, perpetually waiting for a third person to die or divorce. I was afraid of losing her. That summer, she had travelled without me to America (so much farther from Europe then than it is today), and she had come back with a different coloration to her manner, a glaze of independence, as though she had been exposed to a new kind of sun.

I remember how she stared at Magdalena with gentle astonishment, as if Magdalena were a glossy illustration that could not look back. Magdalena had on a pale dress of some soft, floating stuff, and a pillbox hat tied on with a white veil, and long white gloves. I saw her through Juliette's eyes, and I thought what Juliette must be thinking: Where does Magdalena think we're taking her? To a wedding? Handing her into the front seat, I had shut the door on her skirt. I wondered if she had turned into one of the limp, pliant women whose clothes forever catch.

It was Juliette's custom to furnish social emptiness with some rattling anecdote about her own activities. Guests were often grateful. Without having to cast far, they could bring up a narrative of their own, and the result was close to real conversation. Juliette spoke of her recent trip. She said she was wearing an American dress made of a material called cotton seersucker. It washed like a duster and needed next to no ironing.

For answer, she received a side view of Magdalena's hat and a blue eye shadowed with paler blue. Magdalena was not looking but listening, savoring at close quarters the inflections of the French Protestant gentry. She knew she was privileged. As a rule, they speak only to one another. Clamped to gearshift and wheel, I was absolved of the need to comment. My broken profile had foxed Magdalena at first. She had even taken me for an impostor. But then the remembered face of a younger man slid over the fraud and possessed him.

Juliette had combed through the *Guide Michelin* and selected a restaurant with a wide terrace and white umbrellas, set among trees. At some of the tables there were American officers, in uniform, with their families—this is to show how long ago it was. Juliette adjusted our umbrella so that every inch of Magdalena was in shade. She took it for granted that my wife belonged to a generation sworn to paleness. From where I was sitting, I could see the interior of the restaurant. It looked cool and dim, I thought, and might have been better suited to the soft-footed conversation to come.

I adjusted my reading glasses, which Magdalena had never seen, and stared at a long handwritten menu. Magdalena made no move to examine hers. She had all her life let men decide. Finally, Juliette wondered if our guest might not like to start with asparagus. I was afraid the asparagus would be canned. Well, then, said Juliette, what about melon. On a hot day, something cool followed by cold salmon. She broke off. I started to remove my glasses, but Juliette reminded me about wine.

Magdalena was engaged in a ritual that Juliette may not have seen before and that I had forgotten: pulling off her tight, long gloves finger by finger and turning her rings right side up. Squeezed against a great sparkler of some kind was a wedding ring. Rallying, Juliette gave a little twitch to the collar of the washable seersucker and went on about America. In Philadelphia, a celebrated Pentecostal preacher had persuaded the Holy Spirit to settle upon a member of the congregation, a woman whose hearing had been damaged when she was brained by a flying shoe at a stock-car race. The deaf woman rose and said she could hear sparrows chirping in High German, on which the congregation prayed jubilant thanks.

Juliette did not stoop to explain that she was no Pentecostalist. She mentioned the Holy Spirit as an old acquaintance of her own class and background, a cultivated European with an open mind.

We were no longer young lovers, and I had heard this story

several times. I said that the Holy Spirit might find something more useful to attend to than a ruptured eardrum. We were barely ten years out of a disastrous war. All over the world, there were people sick, afraid, despairing. Only a few days before, the President of Brazil had shot himself to death.

Juliette replied that there were needs beyond our understanding. "God knows what he wants," she said. I am sure she believed it.

"God wanted Auschwitz?" I said.

I felt a touch on my arm, and I looked down and saw a middle-aged hand and a wedding ring.

With her trained inclination to move back from rising waters, Juliette made the excuse of a telephone call. I knew that her brief departure was meant to be an intermission. When she came back, we would speak about other things. Magdalena and I sat quietly, she with her hand still on my arm, as if she had finally completed a gesture begun a long time before. Juliette, returning, her eyes splashed with cold water, her dark hair freshly combed, saw that I was missing a good chance to bring up the divorce. She sat down, smiled, picked up her melon spoon. She was working hard these days, she said. She was translating an American novel that should never have been written. (Juliette revealed nothing more about this novel.) From there, she slid along to the subject of drastic separations—not so much mine from Magdalena as divorcement in general. Surely, she said, a clean parting was a way of keeping life pleasant and neat? This time, it was Magdalena's hearing that seemed impaired, and the Holy Spirit was nowhere. The two women must have been thinking the same thing at that moment, though for entirely different reasons: that I had forfeited any chance of divine aid by questioning God's intentions.

It was shortly before her removal to the hospital that Magdalena learned about Juliette's death. One of her doddering friends may have seen the notice in a newspaper. She at once resumed

her place as my only spouse and widow-to-be. In fact, she had
never relinquished it, but now the way back to me shone clear.
The divorce, that wall of pagan darkness, had been torn down
and dispersed with the concubine's ashes. She saw me delivered
from an adulterous and heretical alliance. It takes a convert to
think "heretical" with a straight face. She could have seen
Juliette burned at the stake without losing any sleep. It is another
fact about converts that they make casual executioners.

She imagined that I would come to her at once, but I went
nowhere. Juliette had asked to be cremated, thinking of the
purification of the flame, but the rite was accomplished by
clanking, hidden, high-powered machinery that kept starting and
stopping, on cycle. At its loudest, it covered the voice of the
clergyman, who affirmed that Juliette was eying us with great
good will from above, and it prevailed over Juliette's favorite
recordings of Mozart and Bach. Her ashes were placed in a
numbered niche that I never saw, for at some point in the funeral
service I lost consciousness and had to be carried out. This
nightmare was dreamed in the crematorium chapel of Père
Lachaise cemetery. I have not been back. It is far from where I
live, and I think Juliette is not there, or anywhere. From the
moment when her heart stopped, there has been nothing but
silence.

L ast winter, I had bronchitis and seldom went out. I managed
to send Magdalena a clock, a radio, an azalea, and enough
stamps and stationery to furnish a nineteenth-century literary
correspondence. Nevertheless, the letters that reached my sick-
bed from hers were scrawled in the margins of newspapers, torn
off crookedly. Sometimes she said her roommate had lent her the
money for a stamp. The message was always the same: I must not
allow my wife to die in a public institution. Her pink-nosed
woman friends wrote me, too, signing their alien names,
announcing their titles—there was a princess.

It was no good replying that everybody dies in hospital now. The very idea made them sick, of a sickness beyond any wasting last-ditch illusion. Then came from Magdalena "On Saturday at nine o'clock, I shall be dressed and packed, and waiting for you to come and take me away."

Away from the hospital bed? It took weeks of wangling and soft-soaping and even some mild bribery to obtain it. Public funds, to which she is not entitled, and a voluntary contribution from me keep her in it. She has not once asked where the money comes from. When she was young, she decided never to worry, and she has kept the habit.

I let several Saturdays go by, until the folly had quit her mind. Late in April I turned up carrying a bottle of Krug I had kept on ice until the last minute and some glasses in a paper bag. The woman who shares her room gave a great groan when she saw me, and showed the whites of her eyes. I took this to mean that Magdalena had died. The other bed was clean and empty. The clock and the radio on the table had the look of objects left behind. I felt shock, guilt, remorse, and relief, and I wondered what to do with the wine. I turned, and there in the doorway stood Magdalena, in dressing gown and slippers, with short white hair. She shuffled past me and lay on the bed with her mouth open, struggling for breath.

"Shouldn't I ring for a nurse?" I said, unwrapping the bottle.

"No one will come. Open the champagne."

"I'd better fetch a nurse." Instead, I made room on the table for the glasses. I'd brought three, because of the roommate.

Magdalena gasped, "Today is my birthday." She sat up, apparently recovered, and got her spectacles out from under the pillow. Leaning toward me, she said, "What's that red speck on your lapel? It looks like the Legion of Honor."

"I imagine that's what it is."

"Why?" she said. "Was there a reason?"

"They probably had a lot to give away. Somebody did say something about 'cultural enrichment of the media.'"

"I am glad about the enrichment," she said. "I am also very happy for you. Will you wear it all the time, change it from suit to suit?"

"It's new," I said. "There was a ceremony this morning." I sat down on the shaky chair kept for visitors, and with a steadiness that silenced us both I poured the wine. "What about your neighbor?" I said, the bottle poised.

"Let her sleep. This is a good birthday surprise."

I felt as if warm ashes were banked round my heart, like a residue of good intentions. I remembered that when Magdalena came back to Paris after the war, she found her apartment looted, laid waste. One of the first letters to arrive in the mail was from me, to say that I was in love with a much younger woman. "If it means anything at all to you," I said, the coals glowing brighter, "if it can help you to understand me in any way—well, no one ever fascinated me as much as you." This after only one glass.

"But, perhaps, you never loved me," she said.

"Probably not," I said. "Although I must have."

"You mean, in a way?" she said.

"I suppose so."

The room became so quiet that I could hear the afternoon movie on television in the next room. I recognized the voice of the actor who dubs Robert Redford.

Magdalena said, "Even a few months ago this would have been my death sentence. Now I am simply thankful I have so little time left to wander between 'perhaps' and 'probably not' and 'in a way.' A crazy old woman, wringing my hands."

I remembered Juliette's face when she learned that her menopause was irreversible. I remember her shock, her fright, her gradual understanding, her storm of grief. She had hoped for children, then finally a child, a son she would have called "Thomas." "Your death sentence," I said. "Your death sentence. What about Juliette's life sentence? She never had children. By the time I was able to marry her, it was too late."

"She could have had fifteen children without being married," said Magdalena.

I wanted to roar at her, but my voice went high and thin. "Women like Juliette, people like Juliette, don't do that sort of thing. It was a wonder she consented to live with me for all those years. What about her son, her Thomas? I couldn't even have claimed him—not legally, as long as I was married to you. Imagine him, think of him, applying for a passport, finding out he had no father. Nothing on his birth certificate. Only a mother."

"You could have adopted Thomas," said Magdalena. "That way, he'd have been called by your name."

"I couldn't—not without your consent. *You* were my wife. Besides, why should I have to adopt my own son?" I think this was a shout; that is how it comes back to me. "And the inheritance laws, as they were in those days. Have you ever thought about that? I couldn't even make a will in his favor."

Cheek on hand, blue eyes shadowed, my poor, mad, true, and only wife said, "Ah, Édouard, you shouldn't have worried. You know I'd have left him all that I had."

It wasn't the last time I saw Magdalena, but after that day she sent no more urgent messages, made no more awkward demands. Twice since then, she has died and come round. Each time, just when the doctor said, "I think that's it," she has squeezed the nurse's hand. She loves rituals, and she probably wants the last Sacraments, but hospitals hate that. Word that there is a priest in the place gets about, and it frightens the other patients. There are afternoons when she can't speak and lies with her eyes shut, the lids quivering. I hold her hand, and feel the wedding ring. Like the staunch little widows, I call her "Lena," and she turns her head and opens her eyes.

I glance away then, anywhere—at the clock, out the window. I have put up with everything, but I intend to refuse her last imposition, the encounter with her blue, enduring look of pure love.

THE ASSEMBLY

M. Alexandre Caisse, civil servant, employed at the Ministry of Agriculture, bachelor, thanked the seven persons sitting in his living room for having responded to his mimeographed invitation. Actually, he had set chairs out for fifteen.

General Portoret, ret., widower, said half the tenants of the building had already left for their summer holiday.

Mme. Berthe Fourneau, widow, no profession, said Parisians spent more time on vacation than at work. She could remember when two weeks in Brittany seemed quite enough.

M. Louis Labarrière, author and historian, wife taking the cure at Vichy, said that during the Middle Ages Paris had celebrated 230 religious holidays a year.

M. Alberto Minazzoli, industrialist, wife thought to be living in Rome with an actor, said that in his factories strikes had replaced religious feasts. (All smiled.)

Dr. Edmond Volle, dental surgeon, married, said he had not taken a day off in seven years.

Mme. Volle said she believed a wife should never forsake her husband. As a result, she never had a holiday either.

Mlle. de Renard's aunt said it depended on the husband. Some could be left alone for months on end. Others could not. (No one knew Mlle. de Renard's aunt's name.)

M. Alexandre Caisse said they had all been sorry to hear Mlle. de Renard was not feeling well enough to join them.

Mlle. de Renard's aunt said her niece was at this moment under sedation, in a shuttered room, with cotton stuffed in her ears. The slightest sound made her jump and scream with fright.

General Portoret said he was sure a brave woman like Mlle. de Renard would soon be on her feet again.

Mme. Berthe Fourneau said it was probably not easy to forget after one had been intimately molested by a stranger.

Mlle. de Renard's aunt said her niece had been molested, but not raped. There was an unpleasant story going around.

M. Labarrière had heard screaming, but had supposed it was someone's radio.

M. Minazzoli had heard the man running down five flights of stairs. He thought it was a child playing tag.

Mme. Volle had been the first to arrive on the scene; she had found Mlle. de Renard, collapsed, on the fifth-floor landing, her purse lying beside her. The man had not been after money. The stranger, described by his victim as French, fair, and blue-eyed, had obviously crept in from the street and waited for Mlle. de Renard to come home from vesper service.

General Portoret wondered why Mlle. de Renard had not run away the minute she saw him.

Mlle. de Renard's aunt said her niece had been taken by surprise. The man looked respectable. His expression was sympathetic. She thought he had come to the wrong floor.

Mme. Berthe Fourneau said the man must have known his victim's habits.

Dr. Volle said it was simply the cunning of the insane.

M. Labarrière reminded them that the assault of Mlle. de

Renard had been the third in a series: there had been the pots of ivy pilfered from the courtyard, the tramp found asleep in the basement behind the hot-water boiler, and now this.

Mme. Berthe Fourneau said no one was safe.

Mme. Volle had a chain-bolt on her door. She kept a can of insect spray conveniently placed for counteraggression.

M. Alexandre Caisse had a bronze reproduction of "The Dying Gaul" on a table behind the door. He never answered the door without first getting a good grip around the statue's waist.

Mlle. de Renard's aunt said her niece had been too trusting, even as a child.

M. Minazzoli said his door was fully armored. However, the time had come to do something about the door at the entrance to the building. He hoped they would decide, now, once and for all, about putting in an electronic code-lock system.

M. Alexandre Caisse said they were here to discuss, not to decide. The law of July 10, 1965, regulating the administration of cooperatively owned multiple dwellings, was especially strict on the subject of meetings. This was an assembly.

M. Minazzoli said one could arrive at a decision at an assembly as well as at a meeting.

M. Alexandre Caisse said anyone could get the full text of the law from the building manager, now enjoying a photo safari in Kenya. (Having said this, M. Caisse closed his eyes.)

Mlle. de Renard's aunt said she wanted one matter cleared up, and only one: her niece had been molested. She had not been raped.

Mme. Berthe Fourneau wondered how much Mlle. de Renard could actually recall.

Mlle. de Renard's aunt said her niece had given a coherent account from the beginning, an account from which she had never wavered. The man had thrown her against the wall and perpetrated something she called "an embrace." Her handbag had fallen during the struggle. He had run away without stopping to pick it up.

Dr. Volle said it proved the building was open to madmen.

M. Alexandre Caisse asked if anyone would like refreshments. He could offer the ladies a choice of tonic water or bottled lemon soda. The gentlemen might like something stronger. (All thanked him, but refused.)

M. Minazzoli supposed everyone knew how the electronic code system worked and what it would cost.

Mme. Berthe Fourneau asked if it would keep peddlers out. The place was infested with them. Some offered exotic soaps, others ivory trinkets. The peddlers had one thing in common—curly black hair.

M. Labarrière said the tide of color was rising in Paris. He wondered if anyone had noticed it in the Métro. Even in the first-class section you could count the white faces on one hand.

Mme. Volle said it showed the kind of money being made, and by whom.

Black, brown, and yellow, said M. Labarrière. He felt like a stranger in his own country.

Dr. Volle said France was now a doormat for the riffraff of five continents.

M. Alexandre Caisse said the first thing foreigners did was find out how much they could get for free. Then they sent for their families.

General Portoret had been told by a nurse that the hospitals were crammed with Africans and Arabs getting free operations. If you had the bad luck to be white and French you could sit in the waiting room while your appendix burst.

M. Minazzoli said he had flown his mother to Paris for a serious operation. He had paid every centime himself. His mother had needed to have all her adrenalin taken out.

Mme. Volle said when something like that happened there was no such thing as French or foreign—there was just grief and expense.

M. Alexandre Caisse said it was unlikely that a relative of M. Minazzoli would burden the taxpaying community. M. Minazzoli probably knew something about paying taxes, when it came to that. (All laughed gently.)

Mlle. de Renard's aunt said all foreigners were not alike.

General Portoret had commanded a regiment of Montagnards forty years before. They had been spunky little chaps, loyal to France.

M. Labarrière could not understand why Mlle. de Renard had said her attacker was blue-eyed and fair. Most molested women spoke of "the Mediterranean type."

General Portoret wondered if his Montagnards had kept up their French culture. They had enjoyed the marching songs, swinging along happily to "Sambre et Meuse."

M. Minazzoli said in case anyone did not understand the code-lock system, it was something like a small oblong keyboard. This keyboard, affixed to the entrance of the building just below the buzzer one pressed in order to release the door catch, contained the house code.

Mme. Berthe Fourneau asked how the postman was supposed to get in.

M. Labarrière knew it was old-fashioned of him, but he thought a house phone would be better. It was somehow more dignified than all these codes and keyboards.

M. Minazzoli said the code system was cheaper and very safe. The door could not be opened unless the caller knew what the code was, say, J-8264.

Mme. Berthe Fourneau hoped for something easier to remember—something like A-1111.

M. Labarrière said the Montagnards had undoubtedly lost all trace of French culture. French culture was dying everywhere. By 2500 it would be extinct.

M. Minazzoli said the Lycée Chateaubriand was still flourishing in Rome, attended by sons and daughters of the nobility.

Mme. Volle had been told that the Lycée Français in London accepted just anyone now.

Mme. Berthe Fourneau's daughter had spent an anxious au pair season with an English family in the 1950s. They had the curious habit of taking showers together to save hot water.

M. Alexandre Caisse said the hot-water meters in the building needed to be checked. His share of costs last year had been enough to cover all the laundry in Paris.

Mme. Berthe Fourneau said a washing machine just above her living room made a rocking sound.

Mme. Volle never ran the machine before nine or after five.

Mme. Berthe Fourneau had been prevented at nine o'clock at night from hearing the President of the Republic's television interview about the domestic fuel shortage.

M. Minazzoli said he hoped all understood that the security code was not to be mislaid or left around or shared except with a trusted person. No one knew nowadays who might turn out to be a thief. Not one's friends, certainly, but one knew so little about their children.

Mlle. de Renard's aunt wondered if anyone recalled the old days, when the concierge stayed in her quarters night and day like a watchdog. It had been better than a code.

M. Labarrière could remember how when one came in late at night one would call out one's name.

General Portoret, as a young man—a young lieutenant, actually—had given his name as "Jack the Ripper." The concierge had made a droll reply.

M. Alexandre Caisse believed people laughed more easily then.

General Portoret said that the next day the concierge had complained to his mother.

Dr. Volle envied General Portoret's generation. Their pleasures had been of a simple nature. They had not required today's thrills and animation.

M. Labarrière knew he was being old-fashioned, but he did object to the modern inaccurate use of *animation*. Publications from the mayor's office spoke of "animating" the city.

M. Minazzoli could not help asking himself who was paying for these glossy full-color handouts.

Dr. Volle thought the mayor was doing a good job. He

particularly enjoyed the fireworks. As he never took a holiday the fireworks were about all he had by way of entertainment.

M. Labarrière could recall when the statue of the lion in the middle of Place Denfert-Rochereau had been painted the wrong shade. Everyone had protested.

Mlle. de Renard's aunt had seen it—brilliant iridescent coppery paint.

M. Labarrière said no, a dull brown.

Dr. Volle said that had been under a different administration.

General Portoret's mother had cried when she was told that he had said "Jack the Ripper."

Mlle. de Renard's aunt did not understand why the cost of the electronic code system was to be shared out equally. Large families were more likely to wear out the buttons than a lady living alone.

M. Alexandre Caisse said this was an assembly, not a meeting. They were all waiting for the building manager to return from Kenya. The first thing M. Caisse intended to have taken up was the cost of hot water.

Mlle. de Renard's aunt reminded M. Caisse that it was her grandfather, founder of a large Right Bank department store, who had built this house in 1899.

M. Labarrière said there had been a seventeenth-century convent on the site. Tearing it down in 1899 had been an act of vandalism that would not be tolerated today.

General Portoret's parents had been among the first tenants. When he was a boy there had been a great flood of water in the basement. When the waters abated the graves of nuns were revealed.

Mlle. de Renard's aunt said she often wished she were a nun. Peace was all she wanted. (She looked around threateningly as she said this.)

General Portoret said the bones had been put in large canvas bags and stored in the concierge's kitchen until a hallowed resting place could be found.

M. Labarrière said it was hard not to yearn for the past they were describing. That was because he had no feeling for the future. The final French catastrophe would be about 2080.

General Portoret said he hoped that the last Frenchman to die would not die in vain.

M. Alexandre Caisse looked at his watch and said he imagined no one wanted to miss the film on the Third Channel, an early Fernandel.

General Portoret asked if it was the one where Fernandel was a private who kept doing all the wrong things.

Mme. Volle wondered if her husband's patients would let him get away for a few days this year. There was always someone to break a front tooth at the last moment.

General Portoret was going to Montreux. He had been going to the same pension for twelve years, ever since his wife died.

M. Alexandre Caisse said the film would be starting in six minutes. It was not the one about the army; it was the one where Fernandel played a ladies' hairdresser.

Mlle. de Renard's aunt planned to take her niece on a cruise to Egypt when she felt strong enough.

Mme. Berthe Fourneau and her daughter were travelling to Poland in the footsteps of the Pope.

M. Labarrière knew it was dull and old-fashioned of him, but he loved his country and refused to spend any money outside France.

M. Minazzoli was taking a close friend to Greece and Yugoslavia. He believed in Europe.

M. Alexandre Caisse said sometimes it was hard to get a clear image on the Third Channel. He hoped there would be no interference with the Fernandel, which must be just about starting.

Dr. Volle said he was not likely to see that or any other film. He went to bed every night before ten. He rose every morning before six.

M. Alexandre Caisse said he thought they would all be quite safe if they left, now, together, in a group. (He held the door open.)

Mlle. de Renard's aunt said she thought the assembly had been useful. Her niece would feel reassured.

Mme. Berthe Fourneau said perhaps she would no longer feel impelled to open and close her bedroom shutters the whole time.

Mlle. de Renard's aunt said her niece slept all day.

Mme. Berthe Fourneau said yes, but not all night.

General Portoret said, After you.

M. Labarrière said, Ladies first.

(All said goodbye.)